The Archangel Invasion

By
Marne L Mercer

CHAPTER 1

How We Found Our Way to the Apocalypse

*"AND MICHAEL, THE SEVENTH ANGEL, EVEN THE
ARCHANGEL,
SHALL GATHER TOGETHER HIS ARMIES, EVEN THE
HOSTS OF HEAVEN.
AND THE DEVIL SHALL GATHER TOGETHER HIS ARMIES;
EVEN THE HOSTS OF HELL AND SHALL COME UP TO
BATTLE AGAINST MICHAEL AND HIS ARMIES.
AND THEN COMETH THE BATTLE OF THE GREAT GOD;
AND THE DEVIL AND HIS ARMIES SHALL BE CAST AWAY
INTO THEIR OWN PLACE, THAT THEY SHALL NOT HAVE
POWER OVER THE SAINTS ANY MORE AT ALL.
FOR MICHAEL SHALL FIGHT THEIR BATTLES, AND SHALL
OVERCOME HIM WHO SEEKETH THE THRONE OF HIM
WHO SITTETH UPON THE THRONE,
EVEN THE LAMB.
THIS IS THE GLORY OF GOD, AND THE SANCTIFIED, AND
THEY SHALL NOT ANY MORE SEE DEATH."*

*The Doctrine and Covenants, 88-112-116, Church of Jesus
Christ of Latter-Day Saints*

I awoke on the famous day of "the 11th hour of the 11th day of
the 11th month", when all the rest of the world found peace in
an armistice ending the Great War. I dreamed the night before
of a meeting between the Angel Moroni and the Archangel

Michael, foreshadowing an apocalyptic battle between the White Angels and the Red Demons throughout Russia. And, when I looked out over a snowy field near the village of Tulgas on the Dvina River, many miles south of Archangel, hundreds of Bolshevik soldiers, or "Bolos," as we called them, came charging out of the forest towards our artillery position with their Mosin Nagant rifles blazing and their bayonets pointed at our hearts.

But how, you may ask, did you find yourself in the middle of a battle in Russia, when the whole world had just found peace, after tens of millions of deaths in the first "World War?"

Listen, fair reader, and I will relate the tale of how thousands of soldiers- Canadians like me, Yanks, Brits, Scots, Aussies, Frenchmen, Czechs, Ukrainians, Poles, Italians, Japanese, White Russians and a polyglot of others, joined what, it turned out, became Winston Churchill's effort to kill the infant Bolshevik movement in it's cradle. To put it less succinctly, Churchill said, "I think the day will come when it will be recognized without doubt, not only on one side of the House, but throughout the civilized world, that the strangling of Bolshevism at its birth would have been an untold blessing to the human race."

So how, you may ask, did a young father of 3 from McGrath, Alberta, Canada, a baseball player, a trumpet player, an elementary school teacher and a "Jack" Mormon, end up fighting the Bolsheviks in North Russia? It is a bit of a circuitous journey, but bear with me, if you will, and you may find out how the Angel Moroni and the Archangel Michael are relevant to my story.

As you may be aware, after polygamy was made illegal in the U.S. in the 1860's, many of the Mormons, including my grandparents, moved to Alberta and other parts of Canada in the 1880s. They tried to fight the U.S. federal law, at first, on

First Amendment grounds, but when they lost in the Supreme Court in 1879, many headed north. Unfortunately, of course, the Canucks soon let them know that polygamy would be frowned on there, as well, but in the meantime, a whole bunch of industrious Mormon farmers had dug canals and had turned the area around Mcgrath into an agricultural Garden of Eden.

So, as I grew up at the turn of the 20th century, I knew nobody but Mormons. We learned to work hard in the fields, and though I was called by the church to train to be a teacher in Regina, as a teenager I cared for horses and worked with my dad as a teamster driving wagons carrying produce and freight between the towns in southern Alberta. This experience handling horses and wagons, of course, would come in handy when I joined my best friend Leroy Harris and went off to join the Canadian Expeditionary Force, to do our part for the Triple Entente against the Triple Alliance in the Great War. But before that, I married my teenaged heartthrob, Florence, or Fife, as I called her, and we produced three great young Mormon children. I was a baseball star and a member of the town band, well liked as a teacher and our family was known as being among the most respected original Mormon settler families of the region.

But early on in life, I developed a habit that was a problem for me, as a Mormon, and for my lovely wife. In my teamster wagon runs up towards Calgary, I got in the habit of stopping at roadside saloons, and, in socializing with wagon drivers and other workers, began knocking back the demon drinks, from beer to whiskey, that along with coffee, were verboten, as Fritzi would call it, among the Latter Day Saints. This drinking, and a tendency to get too friendly with young ladies other than Fife, got me into trouble more than once in my young marriage.

About a year before I enlisted, I was just leaving the schoolhouse and students were heading home, when my best friend, Leroy Harris, who I called Roy, and my father, Ammon Sr, drove up in dad's wagon. There was snow on the ground, and my father had a cast on his arm from breaking it earlier in the fall.

"Just the man I wanted to see," he shouted. He was always cheerful when he worked.

"Wanted to see a man about a horse?" I joked.

"About a whole team of horses, actually," he replied. "Your friend Roy, here, has offered to help take this load up to Lethbridge, but my arm isn't up to drivin' this team. Could you make the run this afternoon and come on home tomorrow? Florence and the kids can stay over at our house if you like."

"Well, I'm always up for a drive up to Lethbridge. How're you doin, Roy?"

"Just fine, Am. A couple of the guys from the band are up in Lethbridge and said we can stay with them if you want, seein' as how late we're gonna get in."

"That sounds great, Roy. And Florence will probably feel better just staying at the house. She isn't due for another week or two so she should be alright."

By the time we delivered the load and pushed through the doors of the saloon at the hotel in Lethbridge, our buddies from the McGrath city band were there, whooping it up with the local coal miners.

"Well, if it ain't the Jack Mormons from Magrath. How're you doin, boys?" one of them called out.

"We're thirsty and cold from a snowy trail, partner! Pour out some of that Scotch whiskey!" I quipped.

"Lookin' to spend some that hard earned gold, I

reckon?"

"Right as rain, right as rain. And who are these young ladies?"

"Now be respectful gentlemen. These are no ladies of the night. This here is Myrtle and this is Lizzie, and they both teach at the school here in Lethbridge."

Mytle and Lizzie looked at us alluringly, going along with the joke.

But being the town band leader and a handsome baseball star from McGrath, I had to play along with the flirting. "Well, is that right? I'm a teacher, too, in Magrath. Maybe we can learn something from each other?"

Lizzie bit immediately on my line with "I am always up for learning something new. What can you teach me?"

Trying to help, Roy piped up with, "Well Ammon here is a baseball star and the leader of Magrath's town band."

Lizzie gave me another alluring look quipped, "Well strike up the band, good lookin'! Let's play ball."

So, we drank it up and had quite a time with our friends and the young ladies of Lethbridge that night.

But little did I know that Florence, not due for at least another week, would go into labor that night. Sarah took the kids and Dr Beeman came over and, before morning the third of our little kiddies, Kay Lloyd, was born. And boy did I hear about it for spending the night in Lethbridge when I got home! I felt terrible about it.

Six months later, though, Florence was even more unhappy

with me. When Roy and I returned from school late one afternoon, she was irritated, like she was worried about me flirting with the teachers at school again. She was taking the laundry off the line as Kay lay in his basket on the grass.

"Am… Leroy, did the teacher keep you after school you naughty boys? Why it's almost five o'clock." Florence was always able to let me know when she was upset.

I was serious in my reply, "Actually Fife, more serious than that. You know Hugh Brown from Cardston? He's working for the government now signing men up for the war. Leroy and I were speaking with him today and he would like us to sign up for the Princess Patricia Regiment."

This got her going, of course! "Am, you know you don't have to join up—you're needed as a teacher, and you have 3 kids and a wife to take care of!"

I knew she wouldn't be happy but tried to make my case. "I know, and I take those responsibilities seriously, as you know, dear. But a lot of Canadians will be joining the allies over their fighting for their countries and to defend democracy and, after this war is over, I don't want anyone to be able to call me a shirker. I want my wife to be able to hold her head up and say she is married to a real man not afraid to fight for his country."

She looked like she was going to well up and cry as she replied, "Well, I know that if you have it in your mind to do this, Ammon Freeman, I will have a hard time talking you out of it. But I hope you know that I would rather that the real man I love would stay home and care for his family and not go off and risk his life for king and country."

So, after weighing the pros and cons, I finally decided it was time to regain my reputation and prove my manhood by fighting for my country. And, along with Roy, I signed up with the Princess Patricia Light Infantry Regiment. Soon, after some basic training, we were steaming off across the continent to do our part "over there."

My dear wife and kiddies,

I missed you immediately, Florence, after you waved goodbye from the platform at Medicine Hat. The railroad is taking us along the shore of beautiful Lake Superior. We have had a wonderful trip so far. In every town we pass the spirit of the Canadian people is reflected in cheering crowds and folks giving us magazines, books and fruit. Everyone shakes our hands and wishes us God speed. It is very much in contrast with the attitude in Magrath, where many of the Mormons were lukewarm about this war. The stay-at-homes will be sorry. I believe I have done the right thing by doing my duty.

You have been my rock, dear, and I love you more than you can imagine. My spirits are high, and, though I would give everything to be home with you and the kiddies, I feel I have done the right thing.

Accept all my love, dear, with kisses for yourself and the kiddies until I return.

As ever,

Ammon

When we got to Northern France, however, the patriotic adventure turned into a nightmare. From the English Channel to Switzerland, hundreds of miles of muddy trenches had turned a war of movement into a bloody butcher shop killing tens of thousands of young men daily fighting over a few miles of territory. In the front lines, the infantry, of course, took the brunt of the action, as they went "over the top" to fight through artillery barrages, machine gun fire, barbed wire entanglements and poison gas to win a few precious yards. Yards which were often lost the very next day.

As a musician in my hometown band in McGrath, I got a great assignment in our unit's band, so spent much of my time making music, behind the lines. Occasionally, as a star athlete in the McGrath baseball team, I was assigned as a runner to sprint between units to carry messages during combat. Not as safe as making music, but much better than being ground up in the meat-grinder by going "over the top."

But when we were assigned to the 4th Canadian Division, where I first met then Colonel Edmund Ironside, I finally saw real action in the Battle of Vimy Ridge, which put the country of Canada "on the map" in world military history. Fighting for the first time as a unified Canadian force, instead of filling into British units, we proudly demonstrated what our young country could do, when push came to shove.

We prepared to take a ridge called Vimy near Arras with months of digging communication trenches and tunnels for mines under the German lines. Then, after bombarding the enemy with millions of shells in one of the most powerful barrages to date, our Canadian forces, on Easter Morning, April 8, went over the top. Waves of young Canadians ran up the ridge, with many falling in waves before machine gun and rifle fire and many more charging on.

And, as I told Fife in a letter written later from the hospital, "I was surprised at how the fear and trembling I expected was not there." But before I knew it a "blighty" from Fritzi tore my shoulder open and knocked me to the ground. And somewhere out on the dark and bloody ridge, my best friend

Leroy Harris was hit by a "whiz bang" artillery round that ended his young life. It later put his name on a marble monument on Vimy Ridge memorializing the Canadian heroism in the fight to save France in what came to be known as World War I.

Luckily, my shoulder wound, though leaving a bit of shrapnel in me for the rest of my life, only put me in a field hospital, which may have saved my life. For it was there, as I recovered from the wound, that I met the almost godlike Colonel Edmund Ironside, who changed the course of my future in the Great War, and the rest of my life.

Edmund Ironside, said to be a descendent of English kings, stood 6 foot 4 and spoke 7 languages proficiently, had proved his bravery as an artillery commander in the Boer War, served in India and was a chief of staff planning for the 4th Division at Vimy Ridge. He was deemed "Tiny" affectionately by his men and was the kind of officer who cared for and praised his troops, and surely impressed me as I lay in my hospital bed.

"Fritz got you with a bit of a blighty there didn't he son?" He seemed to really care how I was feeling.

"Yes, sir. But we gave him what for in return, I guess."

"You certainly did, young man! And what's your name soldier?"

"Ammon Freeman, Colonel. From the Princess Pats. I'm a teacher and a teamster from McGrath Alberta."

"That's just fine, young Ammon. You have done your country proud... but say, what's a man who can handle horses doing in the infantry for heaven's sake? We have a dreadful need for more drivers in the artillery. Do you know how many big guns it will take to win this war?"

"I surely heard a lot of those guns at Vimy Ridge, sir and Fritzi's. But sure, I can handle horses and rigs with the best of them."

Ironside turned to his batman and told him to check with an artillery regiment nearby and the rest was history.

My dearest sweetheart, Fife,

This week is the 2nd month anniversary of my big finale in France. It was then we went over the top at Vimy Ridge. Early that day Roy was killed. Tell his folks I am sorry and that he died a hero!

Meanwhile, Fritzi presented me with a nice blighty. It's truly a minor wound, so don't worry your pretty head about it. But nothing makes a fellow realize the importance of life and those he loves until he sees injury and death up close.

I will never forget the sensation of shooting and being shot at. It was nothing like I expected it to be, and I really felt no fear. But what seemed most absurd was that God's noblest creations would waste time and treasure in efforts to kill each other off.

Things really have been at a stalemate for months and it seems nobody really wants this to end. While tens of thousands are dying and suffering, others have never done so well in their life. Neither side is anxious to quit before a final smash up. I hope they soon will have enough to satisfy everybody. I surely have had my fill.

They censor the mail and are soaking guys who say too much, but I suppose a fellow has the right to express his honest opinions. But they really don't want the truth to be known. Yet, one of these fine days I reckon this Tommyrot will be ended and people will learn the truth of what is happening in this war.

But don't worry too much over these things as I am well and if it were not for this Tommyrot keeping us apart, I would not let it bother my head. It may sound selfish and unpatriotic, but I have learned that patriotism is a poor place to invest your time and treasure and expect returns.

You will be happy to know a fine fellow I met at the field hospital, Colonel Ironside, has arranged for me to transfer to the Canadian artillery, since I have skills from handling horses and wagons back in Alberta. Now I will be assigned back with the artillery bases and not on the front lines going "over the top." I hope that will make you feel much more secure about the safety of your sweetheart as we finish up this war against the Bosch.

Love and kisses to all.

Your loving,

Am

The next time I saw (now Brigadier General) Edmund (Tiny) Ironside was on the platform on September 19, 1918, at Kings Cross Station in London. I had transferred to an artillery battalion, got training in England and worked as a driver throughout 1917 and early 1918. Then I was transferred to a new unit, the 16th Canadian Artillery Brigade, made up of 497 mostly un-married volunteers. I got selected as they were short on drivers. I was excited to learn Tiny would be our chief of staff under Major General Frederick C Poole, in command of the allied forces, for a secret military assignment. Ironside's groom, Piskoff, a Russian, joined him on the train's platform, and many of us in the Canadian artillery who served with them in France, gave Tiny and Piskoff a hearty cheer as they joined us on the train we were boarding for Dundee, Scotland. As it turned out, as Piskoff was posted with the Canadian Artillery, I ended up getting to know him during our service in North Russia so I got a birds-eye view of Ironside's activity and leadership throughout our stay.

As the train sped towards Dundee, we buzzed with curiosity about the mission on which we were being sent. Over a bit of rum with Piskoff, who I met heading for the loo on the train, I learned we would be sailing to Archangel, on the White Sea in Northern Russia. When we were in training in Surrey, we were equipped with huge winter weather coats, snow boots designed by the famous arctic explorer Sir Ernest Shackleton, who spoke to us about surviving in the Arctic, and Mosin Nagant Russian rifles (produced by Westinghouse in the U.S. for the Tsar's army) with long fixed bayonets. We had complained about trading our Enfield rifles and Browning automatics for these guns with bayonets which fell off, did not shoot accurately, and "shot around corners." Aboard the train we were joined by Russian officers in khaki jackets and blue pants, French Colonial infantry in their blue uniforms, a battery of French 75 gunners and a Japanese Colonel. It was truly a strangely equipped and manned international force!

Piskoff, later in the voyage, explained that two missions, Syren and Elope, were leaving from Dundee to provide military assistance to guard vast stores of Allied war supplies in Archangel and Murmansk, Russia. With the overthrow of the Czar in the Spring of 1917, and then of Kerensky's socialist government that fall, the Bolsheviks under Lenin were consolidating their hold on Russia. As the treaty of Brest-Litovsk ended Russia's fight against the Triple Alliance in early 1918, many divisions of the German military were freed up to move to the Western Front. The allies feared the Germans, with these reinforcements, could actually win the war. So, though our main mission was to guard war supplies in North Russia and prevent the Germans from taking these ports for submarine bases, other goals were to support White Russian forces battling the Bolshevik military and reestablishing an Eastern Front against the Germans.

The White Russian forces, along with various allied contingents (British, French, U.S.) along with Cossacks, Ukrainians and other groups, were challenging Red Russian military units in Southern Russia and as far away as Siberia and Vladivostok. British diplomats and intelligence agents, like Ambassador Bruce Lockhart and the spy Sidney Reilly, were assisting anti-Bolshevik groups planning an overthrow of the young government, including an attempt to assassinate Lenin.

Meanwhile, in Northern Russia, before we started on our journey, British Generals Poole and Finlayson prepared to occupy Archangel. Using a former Russian naval officer, George Chaplin, as an organizer, a coup against the ruling Bolsheviks was carried out, sending most of them hightailing it on the railroad towards Moscow.

Ironically, the head of the new moderate socialist government in Archangel was a well-known socialist, Nikolai Chaikovsky. He was a utopian socialist in the 1860's as a student in St Petersburg. His followers were known as the "Chaikovsky Circles." In 1887 he moved to the U.S. and started a utopian movement in Kansas, of all places. In 1880, he moved to England. Then he returned to Russia in 1905 and helped build the cooperative movement there. So somehow, George Chaplin (called "Charlie", of course by the Allied troops), managed to recruit this multi-cultural and multi-lingual socialist to form a puppet government giving the allies cover for intervening in North Russia.

This coup was carried out on July 31st, the day before Poole's arrival with 1500 troops including Royal Scots, a French Colonial Battalion, Royal Marines, a handful of US sailors and some Poles. Entering the mouth of the Dvina River north of Archangel near Mudyug Island, the naval group was shelled by the island's large shore batteries. Using some seaplanes and French naval artillery, they silenced the Bolshevik guns and captured the battery in one of the first land, air and sea attacks in history. Captain Dugald MacDougal, of Lockport, Manitoba, flying a Campania seaplane launched off the HMS Nairana, was among 3 seaplanes in this historic attack. After attacking Mudyug Island, MacDougal flew his seaplane over the city of Archangel, at which point many of the Bolsheviks began fleeing the city.

Steaming up the Dvina into Archangel harbor, the allied troops were welcomed by Chaikovsky, the new socialist government and many of the town's more well-to-do residents. Then a group of American sailors in the group, encountering a band of hostile Bolsheviks in the trainyards, grabbed rifles, commandeered a train and chased them out of the city.

But all of this, of course, was happening before we steamed north from Scotland. The 16th Canadian Field Artillery Brigade, with Ironside and about 900 other British and French troops, sailed aboard the *Stephen* (with sleeping room for about 200). We zigged and zagged to avoid Fritzi's U-boats and were seasick for days. Worst still, the famous Spanish flu of 1918, and pneumonia, started taking their toll on our troops. Starting with some French poilus (two of whom were buried in the cold White Sea), the flu spread throughout the ship. Fortunately, our hearty Canadian troops, doing exercises daily on the decks, arrived in Archangel miraculously free of the flu.

We steamed up the Dvina River (which flows from the south into the White Sea) to the port of Archangel. Built hundreds of years before by Peter the Great, Archangel gave Russia a northern port and base for a large timber industry in the region. It was a small city of mostly wooden but some masonry buildings and wooden sidewalks along 5 miles of the main street on the waterfront. One soldier described Archangel as lots of "odd architecture and Byzantine minarets."

Most of the other streets were unpaved. In spring and fall the streets were muddy. Some plaster covered brick buildings painted white or yellow housed government offices and the homes of the wealthier residents. The palatial home of a rich sugar merchant near the waterfront was set up as the Allied headquarters. A 5-onion domed cathedral was the most impressive building in the city, replete with golden stars and an ominous painting of the Last Judgement.

When the 16th Artillery Brigade finally came ashore in Archangel, we were composed of two six-gun batteries of 18-pounder artillery pieces. The 67th Battery was commanded by Major Arnoldi of Toronto. At the time I was a driver in the 67th and we were soon to move upriver on the Dvina to engage the Bolsheviks. The 68th Battery, led by Major Hyde, of Beaconsfield, Quebec, would move up the Vaga River to the city of Shenkursk. Both brigade commanders had served with great distinction in France. We also had signal, medical, pay, dental and veterinary officers added to our units to make us as self-sufficient as possible in the forests of Northern Russia. Both artillery units were under the overall command of 37-year-old Lt Colonel Charles Sharman. Sharman was born in England but moved to Canada to join the Mounties. He served on the Prairies, in the Klondike Gold Rush and in the Boer War (with the 5th Canadian Mounted Rifles). On the Western Front he commanded artillery batteries from 1915 to 1917. Wounded at Ypres, he became an artillery instructor back in England. He carried himself well and was the kind of commander who inspired discipline and confidence in his men.

As artillery battalions, we were joining the rest of the allied forces who had landed in the occupation of Archangel a month before. After the capturing of Mudyug Island and avoiding two ice-breakers sunk in the river by the Bolsheviks, 3 British ships landed 4,500 Yanks (mostly from the 339th Infantry from Detroit, Michigan), the 337th Field Hospital company and the 310th Engineers. The engineers, it turned out, using the Americans' experience building log forts and blockhouses on their own frontier, constructed the line of log defenses that protected our lives through the bitter winter of 1918. Also landing in September were the Royal Scots, the 21st French Colonial Battalion, The Durham Light Infantry and a Liverpool Regiment, as well as assorted support troops who brought our full complement to 13,000 men.

By the time US Ambassador David Francis arrived in Archangel to review the American troops, he learned from

General Poole that George Chaplin, now commissioned by the British military, had organized a second coup overthrowing the mild old socialist, Chaikovsky, and his ministers, so that the allies could run things in the province as they pleased. The ministers had been taken by boat the night before to be imprisoned in the ancient Solovetsky Monastery on an island in the White Sea. This monastery was built in the 1400's, was fortified and became a commercial center, housed the Russian Old Believers in the 1600s, and was defended successfully by its fortress from attacks by the Swedes in the 1500s and the British in the Crimean War.

Ambassador Francis was outraged at Poole's overthrowing the local government (though it was created by an allied plot to begin with) and ordered the government leaders returned to Archangel. In the meantime, however, the townspeople had got wind of the coup, and the streetcar drivers, mostly women, went on strike, bringing transit to a standstill. Fortunately for local commerce and pedestrians, some of the U.S. troops from Detroit happened to be streetcar drivers, and soon the city folk and allied soldiers were riding happily to market and home again.

Tired of General Poole treating the Russians like Indian natives, the British decided to send him back to England, and our favorite general, Edmund "Tiny" Ironside, took command of the expeditionary forces in North Russia. And we fanned out to fight the Bolsheviks.

My dear wife,

We arrived in Russia after a voyage through the North Sea, around Norway to the White Sea. We had no encounters with Fritzi's U-boats, but many of the lads aboard, mostly French, came down with the Spanish flu. We buried several at sea and a number went directly to hospital in Archangel. I nor any of the Canadians were even seasick and did exercises on deck every day to stay fit.

As we have just arrived, we don't know where we will be stationed, but likely it will be safe and sound duty guarding military supplies on the docks of Archangel. Don't you worry or lose sleep about my safety as my duty may be as routine as when I played with the band behind the lines in France.

Russia looks a lot like Canada or the northern U.S., with big rivers and evergreen forests. There are lots of lumber mills and some industry around Archangel and many hard-working villagers in the countryside growing potatoes and vegetables, fishing or logging to make a living. I'm sure we will have lots of tales to tell of the life of the folks here in the "frozen north" when we return home.

With the same love, dear, only greater every day,

Always yours,

Am

Chapter 2

Getting the Big Picture from The Horse's Mouth

As we spread out south from Archangel, we followed rivers and a railroad to form the five fingers of the hand of allied forces defending the region from the Bolsheviks. This massive hand, from west to east, included a finger at Onega, on the White Sea, linked by rail with the port of Murmansk, a base at Obozerskaya, on the railway to Petrograd, the city of Shenkursk on the Vaga River, villages along the Dvina river, and furthest east, Pinega village, on the Pinega River. Separated by swamps and forests, these 5 fronts were even more remote as the winter set in, covering the region with deep snow, sub-zero temperatures and arctic darkness.

Assigned to the 67th Brigade with Major Arnoldi, I would be helping load the horses, the 18 pounders, and all of our supplies aboard barges to head south on the Dvina River. Most of Hyde's 68th would be transporting their guns on another set of barges on the Vaga River, which splits off the Dvina, to the city of Shenkursk. While they would be headquartered in the province's second largest city, with lovely homes, churches and civilized townspeople (some of the wealthy from St Petersburg and Moscow would summer there), we would be stationed in rough little farm and timber villages, camps and blockhouses, on the Dvina River.

So, knowing we would be out in the forest for a while, a handful of us from the 67th did a night on the town in Archangel to "wet our whistles" before we set sail. As we walked down the wooden sidewalks of the waterfront, we saw British and Tsarist officers strutting about in their fancy uniforms and enjoying the cafes and restaurants. Many Brits were deployed to recruit and train White Russian volunteers. But, as it turned out, other than hungry peasants and criminals from the local jails, recruiting wasn't drawing many volunteers. The local Russians, it seemed, were happy to have the Allies fight the Bolsheviks, and leave them to live their modest lives. This left hundreds of British training officers to enjoy the pleasures of Archangel, while we were freezing in the forests, fighting for our lives against the Bolos.

But that night we did have some fun, trying some of the devilishly potent vodka, guaranteed to drive your cares away, and leaving you wishing you hadn't in the morning. But at a well-known Russian cafe called Café de Paris, where we spent our last night in Archangel, we got more than we bargained for.

I entered the café for dinner and drinks with Piskoff, who Ironside had let off for the evening, and Abe Vronsky, from the U.S. 339.th He was a Polish immigrant who spoke English, Polish and a little Russian, who I met while he was driving one of the Archangel streetcars during the strike. Also joining us was Captain Dugald MacDougal, the flyer from Lockport, Manitoba who had piloted his seaplane in the attack on Mudyug Island, and, flying over Archangel, had driven the Bolsheviks out of the city. I had met Dugald, originally back in France, before he moved from the Canadian infantry to the RAF. As we walked in, Felix Cole, the American Consul in Archangel and his Russian wife, Tatiana, seeing we were with the allied forces, graciously invited us to join them.

We looked around and couldn't believe there was a war on with all the gourmet food being served in the café. Both vodka and Scotch, the latter of which the Brits had brought boat loads of, poured like water. Piskoff and Tatiana pointed out the various dishes at surrounding tables explaining what they were. There was zakuski, a Russian hors d'oeuvres, a classic beet soup, borscht, mutton cutlets baked with cabbage, carrots and other vegetables, pancakes stuffed with beef and buckwheat pancakes with melted butter, sour cream and smoked salmon. Other tasty looking dishes included puff pastry tartlets with farmers cheese, aspic with tongue and salted sardines and smelts sauteed in chicken stock with shrimp and mushrooms. Then there was boiled suckling pig in a sour cream sauce, horse radish salt and pepper. Caviar was served with every course, of course! Then desserts included a pie with cherry jam, almonds, sour cream, egg yolks and cinnamon, delicious cheesecakes, cream pudding and French pastries. Those of us from Canada and the U.S. had never seen such a spread!

As we ate, Abe and Piskoff chatted a bit in Russian with Tatiana, who was a dancer when Cole married her several years before.

Then somebody mentioned the trolley strike in Archangel at which Abe gained fame in his unit by driving the streetcar down Troitsky Prospect, the main boulevard in town. He noted that, being a union guy from the union town of Detroit, he felt bad being a scab against a strike.

He went on to tell us about Detroit's great trolley riot of 1891, which he had heard about from his dad. The privately owned Detroit City Railway had angered both its drivers and its customers by the way they treated their workers and the fee they charged for rides. The trolleys in those years were still pulled by horses, and the drivers, paid for 12 hours a day, were often worked 18 hours for the same pay.

The workers formed an Employees Association, inspired by the Knights of Labor movement, pushing for a 10-hour day, for which the company fired 12 activists. Soon the drivers went on strike.

The proverbial horse dung really hit the fan, though, when thousands of Detroit workers from dozens of other unions went on strike. Huge crowds blocked intersections to block trolleys driven by armed strikebreakers.

Soon the strike grew to an insurrection as strikers, and their supporters, built barricades at intersections with lamp posts, trees and upturned trolleys. Rock throwing mobs battled the police until, near evening, 5,000 men, women and children pushed one of the streetcars into the river.

The company asked the mayor to call in the militia, but instead he announced that arbitration between the union and the company should end the strike, adding that he "would be inclined to throw a few stones himself if the company took too long to settle."

They ended Detroit's great trolley riot, and later the mayor pushed, and the city began to build, a municipal streetcar line which would treat the workers more fairly.

After Abe finished his story about the labor history of Detroit, we got a bushel of new information from Felix on why we Allies were here in Russia, fighting with the Bolsheviks. Despite opinions to the contrary of the other British, French and American diplomats, as U.S. Consul, Felix had warned against allied intervention in Russia. He explained that President Wilson himself, hesitant to intervene, had finally conceded to allied (mostly British) requests for a limited engagement by U.S. forces in Russia. This would include assisting the Czech Legion, tens of thousands of Czechoslovakian troops marooned in Russia after the Brest Litovsk treaty. These disciplined troops, seeing the hope of the formation of a new democratic Czechoslovakia after the Great War, were trying to cross Russia on the trans-Siberian railroad to Vladivostok, so they could be shipped back to the Western Front to help the allies win the war. But after being attacked by Bolshevik troops along the way, their journey became a matter of taking control of the entire railroad and fighting their way across the whole continent.

The other goal in President Wilson's "aide memoire" document defining the U.S. role in Russia, was to keep the German's from capturing tons of war materials in Archangel, Murmansk and Vladivostok and in the case of North Russia, to keep the Germans from capturing the ports themselves and turning them into submarine bases. But what wasn't in his message was an approval of US troops intervening to take sides in the growing civil war between the Whites and the Reds, throughout Russia.

The French and the British, however, were not so reticent about taking sides in the Civil War. Early in 1918, British, Canadian, Australian, New Zealand and South African officers met at the Tower of London to begin planning an allied intervention in the Caspian region and the oilfields of Baku. Traveling up from Bagdad, the "Dunsterforce" under Russian speaking commanding officer Major General Lionel C. Dunsterville, attempted to block Turkey and Germany from gaining control of the oilfields of the Caucasus region. Meanwhile, the British and French also supported southern White Russians like the Don Cossacks and General Anton Deniken and his anti-Bolshevik Volunteer Army. At this point, Deniken was fighting his successful 2nd Kuban Campaign capturing regions from the Black Sea to the Caucasus from the Bolsheviks, and the French were preparing to send more troops into the Ukraine. Some felt the White Russians were on the verge of capturing Moscow.

So, Cole concluded, it was under false pretenses in a fool's errand that the allies had sent our troops to North Russia under the guise of re-establishing an Eastern front and protecting our military supplies as part of the Great War. We had actuality been sent, as Canadian and American soldiers under British command, to fight the Bolsheviks and help overthrow their revolution. Soon, as we travelled up the rivers and forests of the Archangel province, we would learn what that meant.

These revelations stirred some lively conversation, but, as we were sailing early in the morning, we soon wished our dinner hosts farewell, and stumbled back to a boat to the harbor at Bakaritza (the port town and railhead across the river from Archangel) where we would sleep aboard the barges before starting up the Dvina in the morning. As we crossed the choppy river in a launch, the last thing we saw was the 5-golden domes of Archangel's cathedral and its mural of the Last Judgement.

My Dearest Wife,

Had dinner with a Canadian from Lockport, Manitoba, Capt Dugald MacDougal, I met in France, who is now flying for the RAF, a Yank from Detroit, Abe Vronsky, a Russian fellow named Piskoff and the American Consul and his wife tonight. Quite the fancy dinner at Archangel's best restaurant. Learned a bunch more about what we are doing up here in Russia.

For a good time, most of the boys drink, of course, and take all the girls offers, and seem to have good times. But I have avoided both, to become the man I have promised to be for you when I get home. I have always told you the truth and want to put the business back in Canada behind us.

Because of you, dear, I am going on the straight and even path, to put an end to my continual series of fool actions to make me more worthy.

I have dreamed several times about being home with you and the kiddies. I am with you at our home in McGrath and out riding with you on the beautiful rolling prairies of Alberta. I especially enjoy the feeling of holding you and the children in my arms again.

I hope this means you and the kiddies are all are safe and doing well and that I will be coming home to you soon.

Your loving,

Am

I crawled aboard the barge at Bakaritza and found a spot to sleep. We had a hundred bails of barbed wire aboard which, with a blanket thrown over them, made an amazingly comfortable bed. With a little light from a lamp on the stern, after writing a letter to Fife, I opened up the Book of Mormon, hoping, perhaps, for some inspiration and solace in my drunken confusion, after an evening in Archangel.

Always interested in the chapters featuring my namesake, Ammon, one of the sons of Mosiah, I opened to Chapter 17 of the book of Alma. In it, Alma was travelling south from Gideon and met Ammon and his brothers. In this meeting an angel appeared before Alma and the sons of Mosiah. Here's what I got out of my reading:

The sons had been giving themselves to much fasting and prayer giving them the spirt of prophecy and revelation, and they were teaching with the power and authority of God.

They had been teaching among the Lamanites for 14 years, many of whom were brought before the altar of God, calling his name and confessing their sins to him.

After leaving their father, Mosiah, they had journeyed and suffered afflictions of body and mind- hunger, thirst, fatigue and "labor in the spirit." They left the land of Zarahemla, taking swords, spears, bows, arrows and slings, in order to survive in the wilderness.

They travelled through the wilderness to the land of Nephi, preaching to the Lamanites. They prayed and fasted in the wilderness to become instruments of God, and to teach the truth to the Lamanites.

Ammon, the chief among the brothers, departed and went to the land of Ishmael, named after the sons of Ishmael, who also became Lamanites. There he was bound by the

Lamanites, as a Nephite, and carried before the king so he could decide whether to slay, imprison or banish him.

The king's name was Lamoni, a descendent of Ishmael. He asked Ammon if he wanted to live in the land of the Lamanites. Ammon replied that he did, and perhaps for his whole life. The king was pleased with Ammon, unbound him and offered him one of his daughters as a wife.

Ammon thanked him, but instead offered to be his servant, and joined shepherds watching the king's flocks. After three days, other Lamanites scattered the king's flocks. His fellow servants feared the king would be angry, but he reassured them they would recapture the king's flocks.

The Lamanites again tried to scatter the flocks and Ammon slung stones at them, killing a few and their brethren came at him with clubs. Ammon took out his sword, smiting off their arms and the rest began to flee.

Carrying the arms Ammon had cut off in the battle, they returned to the king to give testimony.

Having read enough out of my Book of Mormon and reeking a bit of fish and vodka from dinner that night, I slept on barbed wire bale till just before dawn. The mosquitoes gave me quite a going over, but I discovered, to my delight, that bats would dive over me and clear the air. And, in my sleep, I dreamed and heard for the first time from my new friends Michael, the Archangel, and the angel Moroni.

As Moroni appeared before me in the mist, a golden trumpet at his lips, the blaring horn's notes evoked the Old Testament's Joshua and the fall of the walls of Jericho. As he put down his trumpet, he gazed over towards the firs along the harbor edge in Bakaritza. A glaring light like battle flares lit up the sky. A magnificent white angel, like the ubiquitous statues of the Archangel Michael throughout the city, stood before us, a sword in his hand. He spoke like the booming of cannons:

"Welcome Moroni, Son of Mormon, Commander of the Nephites in the battles against the Lamanites, and Angel of the New World. Welcome to my realm… the realm of the Old World. The scene of the great battle in heaven where I, Michael, struck down the Devil from the firmament. As an angel of the New World, you are welcome to join us in the battle against the Red Legions."

"I am here to serve," said Moroni, "the Legions of the New World are here to join you in the fight against this evil. But who are these Red Legions with whom we must fight?"

"The Red Legions are the forces of the Bolsheviks in Russia. When Fanny Kaplan shot Lenin in Moscow on August 30th, the Red Terror began, and the Bolos began arresting and shooting many of our friends throughout the country. But fortunately, our allies from the Great War have joined us to overthrow our enemies and restore the glory of the Russian empire. Let us bless and strengthen the arms of these young men who have come from so far to fight for the freedom of our people!"

As dreams often do, my dream shifted to a scene back in Alberta. Sleet and rain fell as the cornerstone of the new Alberta Temple was laid in Cardston.

I stood with my mother Sarah, father Ammon Sr and my siblings with 2,000 Canadian Mormons gathered to watch the cornerstone laying ceremony. We were standing by my father's wagon and team, loaded with several large pieces of white granite.

Elder McKay spoke to the crowd: "We are gathered

27

*today to lay the foundation for this first temple of the
Latter Day Saints in our settlement here in Canada.
As pioneers come to dig the irrigation canals to
raise up a Garden of Eden out of these prairies, we
are creating a new home for the faithful. We rejoice
and ask the Lord for his blessings on this temple."*

*As he finished speaking, the Magrath band, in which I was
playing trumpet, started up with "Come, Come, ye Saints," as
all the gathered Mormons sang along:*

*"Come, come, ye saints, no toil nor labor fear;
But with joy wend your way.
Though hard to you this journey may appear,
grace shall be as your day.
Tis better far for us to strive
our useless cares from us to drive;
do this, and joy your hearts will swell -
All is well! All is well!"*

*As the assembly sang the hymn, Elder McCay and helpers lay
down the corner stone of the temple on cement they had
troweled below under a canvas canopy to protect them from
the rain.*

*"Why should we mourn or think our lot is hard?
'Tis not so; all is right.
Why should we think to earn a great reward
if we now shun the fight?
Gird up your loins; fresh courage take,
our God will never us forsake;
and soon we'll have this tale to tell-
all is well! All is well!*

*As the assembly continued singing, the rain and sleet came
down even harder and thunder rolled across the Alberta
prairie.*

"We'll find the place which God for us prepared,

in His house full of light,
where none shall come to hurt or make afraid;
there the saints will shine bright.
We'll make the air with music ring,
shout praises to our God and King;
above the rest these words we'll tell,
all is well! All is well!"

As the assembly sang the final verse, Ammon and his father
worked with other men under an a-frame to lift down the final
granite slabs off the wagon onto the muddy construction site.

"And should we die before our journey's through,
happy day! All is well!
We then are free from toil and sorrow, too;
with the just we shall dwell!
But if our lives are spared again
to see the Saints their rest obtain,
oh, how we'll make this chorus swell-
all is well! All is well!"

Chapter 3

Off to Fight the Bolos

A bugle, not a trumpet, blew reveille at 600 hours, October 8,
though, at this time of the year in North Russia, there was no
real sunrise nor sunset. I and several others aboard the barge,
and troops in the nearby barracks, had our last true hot meal
of eggs, potatoes and ham, before finishing loading for the
voyage up the Dvina. Last aboard were the horses for the 18
pounder cannons. By 1200 hours we were on our way.

Before we set sail, though, we had one humorous incident
when the captain of the transport ship *Stephen* came running

up to demand the troops return a variety of equipment stolen from his ship by some of our enterprising chaps for use on our voyage into the forests. He was at least able to get back some of his lost gear.

Towed by tugboats, our 28 dirty lumber barges, 100 feet long and 40 feet at the beam, open to the weather and accompanied by gunboats, carried both the 67th and 68th Artillery, the Royal Scots and many of the 339th Yanks up the gracefully curving Dvina. In Archangel and Bakaritza the river was almost a mile wide, but soon it narrowed to 400-600 yards. As we passed small peasant villages, swamps and hilly fir covered forests, even we artillerymen and drivers held our rifles at the ready prepared to fight off possible Bolo attacks.

On the way upriver we had only basic British rations- bully beef, M&V (meat and vegetables), biscuits and tea. Oh, and a shot of rum a day, of course. And I, as a tried- and-true *Jack* Mormon, couldn't turn down that one benefit of His Majesty's armed forces!

Actually, it was alcohol, tobacco and a little messing around with the local girls in McGrath, which had gotten me in trouble with Florence, in the early days of our marriage. I assured her in my letters home, of course, that I was going to beat my un-Mormon-like habits while overseas, but I had mixed results in these efforts so far.

As we travelled upriver, we learned that no toilets meant doing your business in buckets on deck and tossing it over the side. Some days a whole line of solders would be tossing their buckets in unison. The troops joked that if your shit sank you were healthy, and if not, not so much. Meanwhile an odd Dvina fish with human-like teeth seemed to like it, either way. We didn't go out of our way to catch those fish, of course!

The peasants in their small wood plank and log villages stared blankly as we floated by. Some might have supported the Bolos, others the Whites. Most seemed to just want to be left

30

alone to live their lives, eking out survival by fishing, farming potatoes and simple vegetables and cutting lumber. The villagers lived in a communal system in which plots of arable land around the village were assigned to each family. Due to the cold, the grains were stunted but included rye, oats, flax and wheat. Vegetables included potatoes, cabbage and turnips. Their diet consisted almost entirely of black bread, cabbage soup and salted fish. They also had chickens for eggs and meat, and game like rabbits, quails, wild ducks and grouse. The forest and swamps provided berries, mushrooms and cranberries as well.

The women would spin flax thread and weave cloth in the winter. Each house would have a large brick stove on which they cooked and a samovar to make tea. The stove was so large some of the family (usually the very young and the very old) would sleep on the warm bricks. The homes smelled of fish and abounded with cockroaches, lice (or cooties as we called them) and bedbugs.

Told that the Russians would be eager to be trained to fight the Bolos, Colonel Sharman noted later that one of the goals of the intervention was "the encouragement of the local Russians who were reported as eagerly awaiting the arrival of the allies to organize and fight the Bolsheviks and restore stable government to Russia."

In Sharman's opinion, however, "these expectations were too optimistic. The average Russian peasant was genuinely afraid of the Bolsheviks, if not a Bolshevik himself, but his chief desire was for both sides to go and fight elsewhere and leave him to his comparatively wretched and peaceful existence. As soon as he realized the small size of the Allied force, he was afraid to assist it in view of certain reprisals from the Bolsheviks in the event of his village coming into their possession and, in many cases, this led to active co-operation with the enemy intelligence agents. It was estimated that at various times more than 50% of all the inhabitants of Archangel were pro-Bolshevik."

Fighting the current upstream, our flotilla reached the junction of the Dvina and the Vaga rivers after about 200 miles. The barges at that point split up, with the bulk of Hyde's 68th Artillery heading up the Vaga toward the city of Shenkursk. We in the 67th and 2 18 pounders and their crews from the 68th, headed further up the Dvina.

When we reached the mouth of the Emtsa River where it flows into the Dvina, the 68th crews and their 2 guns were transferred to a smaller barge to travel 30 miles up to the village of Seletskoe. From there they would travel via forest roads for an attack on the Bolsheviks nearer to what we called the Railroad Front. Hyde later told us how that went. He described the forest roads as mere "tracks" rutted with tree stumps, rocks and creeks. "Field" artillery, in the field manuals described as being designed for this kind of terrain, probably had in mind full sized European draught horses to pull the guns, not the small Russian pony-like horses we had available. With harnesses designed for horses 12 hands high, they didn't serve well for the Russian ponies. If you rode one, your feet would drag along the ground! Added to that, each horse came with its owner, who had his own ideas on how to harness him. But finally, after hitching ten or twelve ponies to each gun carriage, you were on your way.

While the 2 guns from the 68th took a shortcut to their goal, we took the long way, chugging up the Dvina, and arrived in at our destination on Oct 13. In the true military tradition of hurry up and wait, however, when we arrived the British commander in that village had, against Colonel Sharman's advice, decided to retreat and spread out a defense line crossing the Dvina between the towns of Kurgomen and Tulgas.

This deployment gave us in the 67th our first combat experience. We set up our guns and lobbed shells all day at 3,000 nearby Bolsheviks and their 3 artillery batteries, while 950 US infantrymen, Royal Scots and some raw White Russian recruits headed down a rough, narrow road through swamps and forests towards the village of Tulgas.

In not as good a position as it could have been, we settled in on a defensive line between Kurgomen and Tulgas through late October. We built a series of log blockhouses and barbed wire entanglements, thanks to the Yank engineers.

In these first days, we fought a series of small engagements with the Bolos, mostly artillery duels. We learned that the yanks were quite green. Most of them had never seen combat having freshly arrived from training at Camp Custer, Michigan. We joked that our Detroit infantrymen, having been trained at an army base named after Charles Armstrong Custer, whose cavalry unit was surrounded and wiped out by savage Indians, didn't seem to bode well for our expedition. Sitting Bull, whose vision foresaw the massacre of the 7th Cavalry, even escaped to Canada after defeating them, before joining Buffalo Bills Wild West Show. But that's show business, as they say!

The Royal Scots with us, and most of us Canadians, had seen service in France, but because of wounds or one reason or another, the Scots had been downgraded to "B category" troops, best fit for service back at the base for light support duty and as clerks. The bravery and stamina of all these lads, however, proved they would all stand up and do their parts when push came to shove in the Russian wilderness.

Most of us Canadians had spent time in the hellhole of the trenches on the Western Front, and when enemy artillery, machine gun and rifle fire got hot, we felt at home. The Yanks, unnerved by artillery fire and combat at first, observed how we reacted under fire and began to get a notion of how to keep their heads low and stay alive.

One of the early lessons we learned was that the Bolsheviks, armed with much heavier artillery, inherited from the Tsar's army, with much longer range, could often bombard us mercilessly while our 18 pounders couldn't touch them. A trick we began to use was to hitch up a team and move at least one gun down one of the many forest roads, closer to the Bolos. We would attack their artillery units with a series of barrages doing some real damage, hitch up the gun, and head back to our lines. Dangerous duty but we kept the Bolos on their toes!

Another tool in our toolbox in North Russia was modest reconnaissance by Royal Air Force planes based at the allied headquarters in Beresnik (at the junction of the Dvina and the Vaga Rivers) and in Obozozerskaya, on the Railroad Front. They were uncrated and assembled in late October. Of the 30 pilots flying in our sector, the majority were Canadians. Many had been trained in England and had little flying time. They flew DH 4 biplanes on the Vaga in the "A Flight" and Nieuport 17s, Sopwith Strutters and RE 8s in the "B Flight" in our zone. As our eyes on the Bolos, the RAF chaps kept busy with some dangerous flying. They carried a few bombs, would strafe the Reds occasionally, but mostly just kept an eye on the enemy's movements.

My friend Dugald MacDougal, from Lockport, Manitoba, who I had known in France when he and I were still in the infantry, spent much of his time at the base in Beresnik, so flew often over our section of the Dvina in Tulgas. Several times we connected in Archangel, as well. I was sorry later to learn that he, like my friend Leroy Harris, did not survive the war.

While the flyers were getting glimpses of enemy troop movements, we rarely saw them at first. But as we lobbed shells at an invisible enemy, we dug in, built our log blockhouses, strung barbed wire and prepared to defend ourselves as the winter moved in. A winter that meant our airplanes' oil needed to be drained and heated between flights and our machine guns needed to be kept in warm shacks before a battle or mounting on the planes. A winter which would freeze hard the Dvina River and the White Sea and leave us stranded in North Russia, hanging on for dear life till Spring. Meanwhile Trotsky, Lenin and the Red Army kept building up their strength, threatening to "bury us under the arctic ice".

But just as the Dvina began to freeze at the end of October, there was a temporary warming in the weather. This meant that the Bolsheviks, with their gunboats and long-range artillery, could make one major assault on our position between Tulgas and Kurgomen. This brought us to when, on Nov 11, 1918, millions of guns were silenced in a world-wide armistice, but our troops in North Russia had just seriously begun to fight.

On Nov 10, the day before the battle, I again read the Book of Mormon before going to sleep. I started where I left off before our voyage up the Dvina, at Chapter 18 of the Book of Alma.

King Lamoni, learning that we had saved his flock, asked his servants to testify as to what had happened.

They spoke of Ammon's faithfulness in saving the king's flock, and his courage and strength in slaying the Lamonites who had scattered his sheep. They said they didn't know if he was the "Great Spirit", but that he could not be killed by the enemies of the king and had great power.

The king replied that he thought Ammon was, indeed, the "Great Spirit" of whom "our fathers have spoken." He asked them where Ammon, the man of "great power" was. The servants replied that he was "feeding thy horses." Hearing that Ammon was preparing his horses and chariots, he called Ammon to him.

Ammon came to him and asked what he desired, and, at first, the king did not speak. But, being filled "with the Spirit of God," Ammon read the king's mind. He spoke to the king, saying that he knew that he was impressed by Ammon because he had defended his flocks and the other servants, killed 7 of the Lamanites with his sling and sword, and cut off the arms of

35

others.

The king, realizing Ammon was reading his mind, was taken aback and asked, "Who art thou? Art thou that Great Spirit ho knows all things?

Ammon answered, "I am not."

The king asked how he had read his mind. He asked him to speak boldly and explain these things, and by what power he had killed and cut off the arms of those that had scattered his flocks. He offered whatever gifts Ammon would ask of him and that he would guard him with his armies, full knowing that Ammon was more powerful than they were.

Ammon began by asking if the king believed there is a God.

The king replied that he did not know what "God" meant.

Ammon asked if the king believed that the Great Spirit, who is God, created all things which are in heaven and on earth.

The king said, yes, he believed that the Great Spirit created all things on earth but did not know of the heavens.

Ammon explained that the "heavens were a place where God dwells with all his holy angels."

The king asked if it was above the earth.

Ammon explained that yes, God looks down on the children of men, knowing the thoughts and intents of their hearts, because he had created all of them from the beginning.

Indicating he believed what Ammon was saying, King Lamoni asked if Ammon was sent from God.

Ammon explained that he was a man, that men were created in the image of God, and that he had been called on by the

Holy Spirit to teach things to these people so they might know what is just and true. A portion of the Spirit was dwelling within him which gave him knowledge of the power of faith and the desires of God.

He then recited history from the creation of the world, of Adam, the fall of man, and events down to the time Lehi left Jerusalem. He also spoke of the journeying in the wilderness, their sufferings, hunger, thirst and travails.

He described the rebellions of Laman and Lemuel, and the sons of Ishmael, and all the events down to the present time.

Though this was taking place in about 90 BC, he also spoke of the plan of redemption, prepared from the foundation of the world, and made known the coming of Christ.

The king then cried out to the Lord for mercy on him and his people.

Then the king was carried to his wife and was laid on a bed and he lay as if he were dead for two days and nights. His family mourned over him, in the manner of the Lamanites, greatly lamenting his loss.

As I dropped off to sleep from my reading, I suddenly dreamed of the Angel Moroni, again blowing his trumpet in a golden light, standing before the forest and the Dvina River. Sounding like the blare of a hundred trumpets, Moroni spoke-

"God is proud of his servant Ammon, come to fight in the great battle at the end of time. Prepare Ammon, and gird thyself with your sword and shield, for tomorrow the armies of the forces of God will face the Red Terror. Be strong, for coming out of the forest, Red Demons in White Robes will appear to strike you down. Ammon, servant of God and warrior of the Latter Days, fight as if the world and the peoples of God depend on

you!!"

*Blowing his horn again, Moroni disappeared in the snowy
clouds in the forest and Ammon's dream faded into darkness.*

The battle we fought the next day, on what became known as
Armistice Day, was in the village of Tulgas. It was similar to
the little villages throughout the Archangel region. It had a
group of small log houses on a hill above a sloping plain down
to another group of log houses, Upper Tulgas. A small
tributary of the Dvina passed between Tulgas and Upper
Tulgas. A mile below Tulgas was a large building used as a
hospital where wounds were treated before the injured were
sent by boat to Beresnik, 45 miles downstream.

We had our Canadian artillery batteries between the hospital
buildings and the main village of Tulgas. The 339th Yank B
Battalion and the Royal Scots were spread throughout the
villages. In the 3 miles between the main village and the
hospital there were about 500 Allied troops.

We of the 67th, with a light mist on the river in the village of
Tulgas on the morning of the 11th, didn't yet see what was
coming. In a shed where we- 23 drivers, a batman, a cook and
our veterinary sergeant- were having breakfast, we heard rifle
fire both in the upper village, and down by the hospital.
Grabbing our Mosin Nagant's with bayonets in place, we ran
out the doors. From the forest nearest our two 18 pounder
emplacements, hundreds of Bolsheviks streamed towards us,
firing as they ran. Colville, one of our last drivers out the door,
was hit and fell dead just outside the shed.

We charged towards the approaching Bolos, firing as we ran.
There were too many of them, and we fell back into the gun
pits. The stream of our fire, as well as one Lewis gun, slowed
the Bolo advance. Meanwhile, Lt Bradshaw, and the gun
crews in the pit, manhandled the guns out of their slits and

turned them180 degrees and loaded them with shrapnel fuse 5, a fast-burning charge meant for close range action. They fired at point blank range into the charging Bolsheviks, killing and maiming many. This broke the momentum of their charge and littered the field with dismembered bodies. Loading again, the gunners fired more shrapnel into the mass of Bolos, covering the field with more blood and flesh. The survivors of the charge retreated to the tree line.

Meanwhile, the "Category B" Royal Scots showed their true worth as 25 of them advanced to help us fight off the Reds. They traded rifle fire and suffered severe casualties in the gun battle. Soon the green Yanks from the 339th, who had been engaged by more of the Bolos in the village, charged up, and joined the fray, adding to the rifle and machine gun fire pushing the Russians into the forest.

In the confusion of the attack on our gun emplacements, we hadn't realized that many of the Bolsheviks had already attacked the 339th in the upper village. Abe Vronsky later told us what had transpired. Lt Dennis and his troops knew immediately they were outnumbered, and they retreated across a bridge into the main village.

Before attacking us, the Bolos, under their commander, a giant named Melochofski, also had been ransacking the buildings near the hospital. Capturing and entering the hospital, Melochofski ordered his men to kill every wounded American and British soldier. Perhaps he didn't know, we mused later, some of the lads were Canadian. But fortunately, for two reasons, he countermanded the order. The British NCO at the hospital, seeing the Bolos were tired, offered them generous quantities of food and rum.

But more convincing, Melochofski's mistress, Olga, a strikingly attractive woman, announced she would shoot any soldier who threatened to kill the wounded. Having allowed the patients to live, Melochofski left his mistress in the hospital and joined the attack on our gun position. Somewhat later, after taking a load of our shrapnel point blank, Melochofski was carried to the hospital, dying in Olga's arms.

Having held off the attack on our gun emplacements and driven back Bolos with machine gun fire from a log blockhouse, we were surrounded by Bolos in the forest, but secure, by nightfall. Just as darkness fell, Lt Dennis took a few men to chase off snipers around the perimeter. At the same time, our gunners bombarded buildings in the lower village where some Bolos had taken refuge, then turned the guns around to lob some shells into the forest to the south. To keep us from calling for reinforcements, the Bolos had cut our telegraph lines.

So as the whole of the civilized world found peace on Armistice Day, we had our first real trial by fire and prepared to defend ourselves from the growing Red Army in North Russia.

We were later proud to learn that Colonel Sharman was told by General Ironside that our action in Tulgas, when we, the drivers, saved the guns from attack, was a rare moment in the annals of British artillery. Having the drivers save the guns had only happened twice, in the Boer War and in 1811. Several of our men received medals for their heroism.

But when the Canadian press covered the Battle of Tulgas, pride for the soldiers' valor was tempered by editorials questioning why Canadians were fighting and dying in Russia when the war had ended. Protecting the military supplies in North Russia and re-establishing the Eastern Front were now moot points. And soon another expeditionary force including Canadians, Americans and the Japanese was moving into Siberia, through the port of Vladivostok. Many Canadians, especially those in the labor movement, were questioning whether we weren't actually there to overthrow the Bolshevik Revolution.

Many of us in North Russia, of course, were beginning to ask the same question.

But the day after Armistice Day, the war was certainly not over for us! At sunrise that day, five Bolshevik gunboats appeared, just out of range of our artillery, and their ten longer range guns pounded us in the village. A main target was the log blockhouse guarding the creek bridge. If they could destroy this strong defensive post, the Bolos in the surrounding forest could charge in again. With mud, straw and debris from explosions clogging up the gun ports, Sergeant Wallace ran outside under heavy machine gun fire and cleared them. Reprising the act when, again, they were clogged with straw, he was severely wounded, earning a Distinguished Conduct Medal from the British.

Finally, a direct hit inside the blockhouse killed everyone but Private Bell, who himself was badly wounded in the face. He kept firing a Lewis gun until dark, when he was finally relieved. He had remained the only one defending the blockhouse, keeping the Bolos in the forest across the stream.

The next day Bolo gunboats continued blasting our positions in the village. They brought several more howitzers to the woods above Upper Tulgas and began, again, attacking the blockhouse above the footbridge. At noon it took a direct hit killing 2 men. The Bolos charged the bridge but were cut off by several Lewis guns, one in the village church. Repeated attacks across the bridge were defeated by more machine gun fire. Finally, on the north side of town, the Royal Scots proved their worth, again, by recapturing the hospital, where all the wounded were still alive. Surprisingly, they were still being nursed by none other than Melochofski's mistress, Olga.

Later in the intervention, "Lady Olga", as our soldiers dubbed her, came to work at the Allied hospital at our base at Beresnik, and later, Archangel. A darkly beautiful and intelligent woman, she had formerly served in the famous

41

Russian Women's Battalion of Death, a corps of 2,000 female volunteers recruited between the February and the October Revolutions. She joined the Soviet cause for adventure, not politics. Then, falling in love with Melochofski brought her to Tulgas. But later, writing home to her comrades, she told them they shouldn't believe the lies their commissars were telling them. She said the Allies were really fighting for the good of Russia.

We were nearly sleepless in the village for three days as the gunboats pounded us and machine guns rattled from the surrounding forest. We were gaunt, drawn, hungry and at our wits' ends. We had to do something as we couldn't go on like this.

In mid-November the Bolos continued to charge the bridge and pound Tulgas with artillery. The rate of fire, at times, began to be reminiscent of the artillery on the Western Front. Shells exploding every 15 seconds reminded us of our time in the trenches at Vimy Ridge.

We finally realized our only hope was to counterattack to dislodge the Bolos. We observed the enemy using charcoal kilns in the trees above Upper Tulgas for storage and observation posts. The Bolos were gathered and bivouacked around these log huts. We decided we needed to assault this position through the woods, in a surprise attack, to convince the enemy we had reinforcements on the way and were still up for a fight.

To lead this charge, a soldier with an unlikely history was chosen. Lt John Cudahy, from Cudahy Wisconsin, was born of a famous midwestern meat packing family, graduated from Harvard and got his law degree at U of W. His several years of practicing law before he joined the Army in 1917 ill prepared him for the bloody battle facing him, but he stepped up to the challenge.

Cudahy, Lt of Company B, which included my pal Abe

Vronsky, and Lt Denham of Company D, led the 2 companies through the woods and crept up to the observation shacks. They savagely attacked, yelling and firing, before the Bolos knew what was happening. Thinking they were being attacked by a larger body, the Reds ran in every direction. Setting fire to the ammunition in the charcoal kilns, the Yanks set off explosions and flying shells convincing the Bolos a full-fledged attack had begun. Continuing into the village of Upper Tulgas, the Yanks expected resistance from the cabins, but the few Bolos left in the village streamed out with their hands up, surrendering to the Yanks, shouting "tovarish, tovarish?" ("Comrade, comrade!). Abe told us later he really got a kick out of this.

The upshot of the battles that began on Armistice Day was our troops had seriously engaged the Bolsheviks inflicting many casualties and driving them further upriver towards their base at Kotlas. We suffered 30 dead and 100 wounded. We estimated that 500 bolos died in Upper and Lower Tulgas. 3 civilians were killed, as well, the village priest and his 2 children, when a shell hit their house.

Worse for the poor peasants (or *moujiks*, as they were called), the officers decided that, as Upper Tulgas seemed to be too friendly with the Bolos, and as it was likely to be captured again by snipers, the troops would have to burn it. The villagers were given 3 hours to remove their belongings, then the flames razed Upper Tulgas to the ground. The sad eyed peasants wept and looked at the Yanks with anger.

Sgt Silver Parrish, leader of the Company B troops who burned the village, felt terrible about it. "My heart ached to have the women fall down at my feet and kiss my hand and beg me not to do it," he wrote later, adding, "But orders is orders." One of the Tulgas locals asked what the Allies goals were in Russia. Were they there to restore the Czar? If so, why burn simple moujik's homes and take their possessions?

We really didn't have good answers. We realized that, as this war proceeded, it would be harder and harder to know our friends from our enemies. It would also be hard to know who we were actually helping by being deployed in North Russia.

In these early battles at Tulgas, it was clear, too, that the Bolsheviks were seriously investing in the fight to defeat the Allies in the forests of the Archangel province. Killed in the battle were three commissars, including the giant Menchofski, Lady Olga's lover. The commander of the Bolshevik forces on the Dvina, a veteran of the Russian Imperial Army, named Foukes, was also killed.

But rumored to have been there as well, overseeing the battle in one of the gunboats, was Leon Trotsky, the Bolsheviks' Minister of War, who famously travelled, often by armed trains, from one battle front to another throughout the Russian Civil War. His being there would indicate the priority Red leadership put on defeating the Allies in North Russia.

Trotsky, his nom de guerre as a Bolshevik, was born Lev Davidovich Bronstein in the Ukraine in the late 1870s. He was a longtime revolutionary but joined Lenin in the leadership of the Bolsheviks in 1917, helping to overthrow the provisional government in the October Revolution. After the treaty of Brest-Litovsk in March 1918, Trotsky began building an almost non-existent Red Army into a force of over 600,000 men by the time they were battling the Allies in Tulgas.

My Dearest Wife,

I know how you don't want to hear about the risks and danger out here, but I am so proud of our Canadian boys for our work in the Russian villages. We, the drivers, saved the guns and gunners from an attack by the enemy.

I can't say more about where we are, and what we are doing, but we are helping defend the villagers in the forests of North Russia. I am working hard to be the brave and responsible husband that you were hoping you married.

Don't worry your head as our boys are well trained well-equipped and we are all hoping and aiming to be home before you know it.

Hugs and kisses to you and the little ones. Be glad you live in a country where the families and little ones are safe, and not in daily danger, as in countries like Russia and in France.

Love and kisses to all, dear.

As ever, sweetheart,

Am

As I finished my short missive to Florence after the Tulgas battle, I found myself restless, and before falling asleep, returned to the Book of Mormon, Chapter 19 of Alma. I remembered that in Chapter 18, King Lamoni had died and lay in bed for two days and nights. Then,

Just as they were about to lay him in his sepulcher, the queen called Ammon to her side. She let him know she had learned that he was a prophet of God and could do many works in his name. She asked him to go and view the body of her husband, as some said he was dead, and other that he wasn't.

Ammon was glad as he knew the king was under the power of God, that a dark veil of unbelief was being removed from his mind and that the light of the glory of God was infusing joy into his soul. This was removing the cloud of darkness and the light of everlasting life had lit his soul. He knew the light had overcome his frame and carried him away in God.

When he returned to the queen, he told her that not only was the king not dead, but that he was sleeping in God, and, on the next day, would rise again. He asked if she believed what

he had told her, and she indicated that she did.

He praised her for her faith, and she spent the night watching over the king until, at the time Ammon had predicted, the king arose.

As he stood up, he stretched his hand to her and said "Blessed be the name of God, and blessed art thou. For as sure as thou livest, behold, I have seen the Redeemer; and he shall come forth, and be born of a woman, and he shall redeem all mankind who believe on his name."

Having said these words, the king's heart swelled up and he and the queen sunk down with joy, overpowered by the Spirit.

Ammon, seeing that the Spirit of the Lord for which he had prayed had flowed upon the Lamanites, fell to his knees and poured out his soul and thanksgiving to God. He, and the king and queen, sank to the earth, overpowered by joy.

Then the servants of the king cried to God, and all fell to the earth, as well. Then, a woman named Amish, who had been converted earlier to the Lord, when she saw the king, queen and servants lay prostrate, ran to tell the people, believing this would cause them to believe in the power of God.

Soon a multitude of the people entered the room and began arguing about the meaning of what they saw. Some thought that having Ammon, a Nephite, among them was a great evil. Some were angry with Ammon for the men he had killed in guarding the king's flock.

One in the crowd, whose brother had been killed by Ammon's sword, drew his sword and approached Ammon to kill him. But as he lifted his sword, he fell dead. When the multitude saw this, they were afraid and wondered what was the great power that had caused the man to die.

When the multitude saw the man had fallen dead, they were

full of fear, and marveled at the great power that had saved Ammon. Some said he must be the Great Spirit and others that he was sent by the Great Spirit. But others rebuked those who had spoken, saying Ammon was a monster, sent by the Nephites to torment them.

As the arguments continued, the woman who had alerted the multitude was sorrowful about the contention, shedding many tears. She took the queen by the hand and cried, "O blessed Jesus, who has saved me from an awful hell! O blessed God, have mercy on this people!"

She then clasped her hands, filled with joy, speaking words which couldn't be understood, then took the king by his hand and he rose to his feet.

The king chastised the arguing multitude, teaching them about the Great Spirit as he had learned from Ammon, and many of them were converted to believe in the Lord.
But others rejected his words and went away.

Ammon arose and spoke as well, as did the servants of Lamoni, saying their hearts had been changed. Many declared that they had seen angels and conversed with them, learning about God and his righteousness. Hearing this, many in the crowd were baptized, became righteous and established a church.

And, nearing sleep, Ammon read the last words of Chapter 19:

"And thus the work of the Lord did commence among the Lamanites; thus the Lord did begin to pour his Spirit upon them; and we see that his arm is extended to all people who will repent and believe in his name."

Chapter 4

Chasing the Bolos Down the Railroad Front

Months before the Battle of Tulgas, on August 2, the British

General Poole had first come ashore with Scottish bagpipes wailing and streamers flying to the cheers of the bourgeois residents of Archangel and to meet the newly victorious Chaikovsky and his Socialist cabinet. The Bolsheviks in Archangel were pretty much either captured or on their way out of town. The next day, the first Americans to see action in Archangel were a group of "bluejackets", American sailors from the *Olympia*, who had been guarding the railroad yards. A group of Bolos had headed south from the yards on a train and the sailors commandeered a locomotive which was fired up and ready go. In a race out of Buster Keaton in *The General*, they barreled 30 miles down the southbound track firing at the Bolos. When an engine malfunction stopped them, the Bolos burned the bridge in between them and the Yanks and prepared to fight. As they dug in, the Yanks started to try and swim the river but intense fire by the Russians drove them back behind the flat cars for cover.

This force of 25 sailors under Ensign Hicks began the first southbound combat against the Bolsheviks, not part of President Wilson's Aide Memoire on intervention in North Russia, but fully fitting with the Brits plan of engaging against the Bolsheviks and their dream of world revolution. With additional French and Royal Scots, this spontaneous incident became the beginning of the Railroad Front that would tie up many allied troops throughout the winter. Ensign Hicks, too, had the honor of taking a bullet in the leg, becoming the first casualty of the Allied intervention

Colonel Guard, head of the "A" force, which did early fighting on the Railroad Front, set the tone for the fighting there. "All patrols must be aggressive and it must be impressed on all ranks that we are fighting an offensive war, and not a defensive one, although for the time being it is the duty of everybody to get the present area in a sound state of defense. All posts must be held to the last as we do not intend to give up any ground which we have made good."

Moving south on the railway, General Poole put the French

Colonial Battalion to work testing the Bolos defenses but was making little progress. The poilus, from their many months in the French trenches, had gained a healthy respect for machine gun emplacements, and moved forward with caution. But they made some progress towards their ultimate goal, Vologda, 400 miles south of Archangel, on the railway. This would help fulfill the ambitious strategy of linking with the White Russians and Czech Legionnaires as they fought their way west on the Trans Siberian Railway (they were now as far as Viatka). Meanwhile, the Royal Scots would also need to capture Kotlas, 500 miles southeast of Archangel on the Dvina River. But as the two fronts, the Dvina and the Railroad, were pushed forward, they diverged, putting more and more distance between the allied fighting units.

On September 5th, the 21st French Colonial Battalion pushed through to the key crossroads railway station at Obozerskaya, soon to be the allied headquarters on the Railroad Front. A tall water tower marked the station and served as an artillery spotter platform looking up and down the tracks and out along trails and roads into the forest to the east and west. A Union Jack was already flying from the train station and greeted the 3rd Battalion of the 339th as the Yanks arrived the next day. The surrounding village was log cabins and shacks, with large piles of firewood cut for the locomotives being stacked to form barricades against attack.

The newly arrived Yanks marched under gray skies and rain from the train to Verst 466 (a verst is a measurement in Russia equal to about 2/3 of a mile). A French officer began waving at them frantically and their Major, Charles Young, stared back blankly, until exploding artillery shells let them know they were under a barrage by the Bolsheviks. They ran to the forest line and into the swamp. When the firing ended Young ordered them not to light fires as they jealously watched nearby poilus drying bits of their clothing on sticks over fires.

After this introduction to Bolo artillery, the Yanks settled in on the Verst 466 defensive line. Two days later, they experienced another first as 2 Bolshevik biplanes flew in and dropped bombs on their position. Circling for a return run, one of the planes lost power and glided to a crash landing in a field several hundred yards from the Yanks. Major Young, somehow mistaking them for British flyers, ran towards the grounded plane yelling "Don't shoot! We are Americans.!" The Russian pilot, uninjured in the crash, fired off a salvo from his machine gun sending Young diving for cover. After the Bolo flyers disappeared into the forest, several of Young's men ran out to recover what they thought would be their Major's body. They ended up helping him get up and brush the moss from his body. As it turned out, only his pride and self-respect were injured in the incident. A few days later, Major Young was reassigned to the provost's office in Archangel due to his less than insightful combat leadership skills. In response to this humorous incident, "Don't shoot! We are Americans!" became a running joke among the Yanks on the Railroad Front.

When the Reds earlier took Obozerskaya, many of the villagers had fled. As the Allied base there grew, however, they began returning, sharing their modest homes with the soldiers and augmenting their income by hitching up horses to their droshkys to haul equipment, cutting wood and performing other services for the troops. Sometimes they would trade vegetables for tobacco, bully beef or crackers.

As the most important regional allied base in the province, Obozerskaya grew throughout the winter. This was the transport and supply headquarters, as well as the railroad repair yard. An airfield was cleared nearby and buildings were built or requisitioned for troop housing and medical facilities.

Our most important tools in the Railroad Front toolbox were our armored trains. The first was a train with naval artillery guns mounted on the coal car, surrounded by piles of sandbags. Preceding this was a car similarly loaded with sandbags but armed with machine and Lewis guns. The armored train's gunners were motley Poles and Russians under British sergeants and a one-armed veteran of the Western Front, also named Young. At night the train parked next to the blue British headquarters train, flying its Union Jack, in the station in Obozerskaya. The allied armored train had its counterpart in Bolshevik artillery trains, of course, which dueled with us as the front moved up and down the railroad

On September 11, the still green lads of Company M got their first chance to see armored trains in action. Riding on the Allied train south, Lieutenant Danley saw what he thought was a long, tall artillery gun ahead, indicating a Bolshevik armored train. Colonel Guard, before going to the rear, smirked and corrected the Lieutenant saying it was just the smokestack on a sawmill.

No sooner had the words left his mouth, of course, than the "sawmill" flashed, a "boom" was heard and an artillery shell whistled by falling into the Allied trenches to the rear. Rather than wait for the Bolo gunner to correct his range, the Yanks charged forward and engaged the enemy successfully, moving the Railroad Front to Verst 464. Five days later, the Bolos counterattacked with machine guns and hand grenades. Two companies, I and L, repulsed the Bolo attack, supported by artillery on the armored train. In this encounter the 339th experienced its first casualties, with two wounded and 3 killed. Soon the graveyard in Obozerskaya began to sprout allied graves.

On September 28, General Finlayson arrived in Obozerskaya and ordered an immediate advance, that afternoon, to attack the enemy's defenses at Verst 458 and 455. The general, of course, was severely handicapped by the same lack of adequate intelligence, especially accurate maps of or guides through the province's forests, as were all the allied forces throughout the winter. He ordered flanking advances by the Yanks through the forest to the right and left of the railroad line, and the French Colonials, led by a veteran of fighting in Africa, Captain Alliez, were brought up to attack directly down the rail line. The flanking units would hike out on lumber roads, first east and west, then turning south, paralleling the railroad, and converge to join an attack the next day at dawn.

The strongest American force, made up of M and I Company troops, and a small team of engineers to blow the tracks behind the Bolos at Verst 455, hiked that afternoon and late into the night on the log roads. Returning west towards the tracks in the pitch dark, they stumbled into a huge marsh. Wandering lost and exhausted through the night, the Yanks got close enough to the Bolo position to hear their locomotives on the track. Realizing the swamp would keep them from reaching their destination, they doubled back, hoping to reach some point on the railway to be of assistance in the attack at dawn.

As the sky lightened, they still had not returned to the rail line, barely able to find a trail back through the woods. At dawn they heard the battle starting with artillery and rifle fire around the Bolo position as the French attacked. Finally, they left the forest back at the Allied armored train, where Major Nichols, having just arrived to relieve Major Young, ordered them to make fires and heat and eat bully beef and hard tack and rest briefly after their night without sleep. They needed to regain their strength as they would soon be moving up the rail line to join the fight.

While M and I company waded in the dark swamps, the French and American machine gun and mortar units attacked following an artillery barrage on the Bolos first trench line. Lt Keith, with 22 men and 3 Stokes mortars, the right flanking Yanks, managed to capture some Bolshevik cabins, first clearing them with hand grenades, and capturing a German machine gun. The Bolos counterattacked on the left, splitting the French and the Americans. They were slowed by mortar fire by the Yanks but were veteran Bolshevik sailors and Red Letts (the Latvians were among the toughest and most loyal Bolshevik troops) and as the mortar shells ran out (due to Colonel Sutherland bringing up insufficient ammunition for the

52

attack) they took back some of the ground they had lost that day.

But the Franco-American force, despite artillery and other fire from the Bolos, held the bridge they had captured. Red artillery shells tore up the tracks, but the bridge still held. The casualties that day, though, were worse than at the earlier railroad fight. The French lost 8 men, killed, wounded or missing. The Americans suffered 4 dead and 14 wounded. Some of the casualties, unfortunately, were not caused by enemy fire, but by Colonel Sutherland's order to put artillery fire on the railroad bridge held by the Yanks, on which the Bolos, 700 yards further south, were also firing.

Meanwhile Sutherland, in an event witnessed by his French interpreter, when learning he was firing on his own troops, before calling off the artillery fire, called for another bottle of whiskey. When he returned to his Blue headquarter train at Verst 466, he feared that the Bolo counterattack and the friendly fire casualties on the bridge meant the Bolos were too strong and ordered a retreat. But Major Nichols and Captain Alliez, not wanting to lose the bridge they fought so hard to take, countermanded Sutherland's order. Then, for three days and nights, the poilus and the Yank M and I companies held onto the 3 miles gained in the battle and kept the Reds from recovering the bridge.

For the next couple of weeks, artillery duels and random patrols filled the days. The Allies and the Bolsheviks were beginning to respect each other as fighters and strategists and took care not to be caught in a battle unprepared. By October 13th, however, it was time again to go on the offensive. M company and the Colonials headed into the woods in a flanking action. Soon the blue-clad French and the olive drab Doughboys were taking shrapnel artillery fire from the Bolos. Reaching their objective, the jumping off point tomorrow for an attack at Verst 455 (the Bolos' rear position), the troops ate and slept till morning. The two French and the 2 American senior officers shared a moss-covered log as a pillow, ignoring the fact that the Engineer officer's pockets were filled with dynamite to use to blow up the Bolshevik's armored train the next day.

Moving out without food or smokes before dawn, the platoons got separated on the way to the railroad and the timing of the attack was thrown off. The sappers who planned to blow up the train were far behind. As the first Franco-American troops got within sight of the Bolo watchtower a wave of Reds well outnumbering them attacked. Within 10 minutes the Allies were in serious trouble, which could be seen plainly by the following platoons. Seeing their brothers were in trouble, the rest of the force brazenly attacked, bugles blaring, shouting and firing. As often was the case, the Bolos were shooting a bit high as the Allies charged out of the woods and soon retreated, climbing aboard their troop train as it headed south along the track. Trying to hold off their attackers with two machine guns, the Bolos took heavy casualties as the combined Franco-American wave continued to fire on them as they rolled down the track.

The surprise attack against their rear position at 455 left the Bolos forward at 457 retreating south into the woods to join their retreating comrades. In the meantime, the allied armored train pulled across the hard-fought bridge at 458, repaired the track and moved down to join the troops at 455. The Red armored train, which had been harassing the Allies in their new position, now got as good as it was giving as the Polish gunners blasted them with their two naval guns.

As signalmen laid telephone lines back from 455 to the former forward base, I Company and more poilus came forward to build on the day's success by attacking the Reds at their new position at Verst 450. By September 15th, the Bolos were driven back to Verst 448 where the Doughboys again dug in.

After fighting with great valor thus far on the Railroad Front, the French became one of the groups which began to object to fighting in this undeclared war in North Russia. The word of an impending armistice in the fighting in Europe began making the troops question why, and for whom, they were fighting. Suddenly, the poilus refused to fight, leaving I company to hold the line on the Railroad Front.

On October 16th, I-Company was now fighting without French help trying to stem the Bolo counterattack on their forward position. Battered by the Bolo artillery, Captain Winslow led an attack in the woods which lasted through the afternoon. I Company, with 1 dead and 4 wounded, dug in, as did the Reds.

The next day, M Company, after rest, food and preparation, planned to come to I-Company's aid. Kept awake by firing between the Yanks and the Reds in the night, M Company marched forward behind a rolling barrage of artillery reminiscent of battles in France. Major Lee had moved the artillery up for a better position during the night. Lt Stoner's platoon charged in, obliterating the Bolos' outpost with intense firing and kept moving till they hit a deep stream. Beyond, they observed a clearing, chopped wood and a woodcutter's cabin and 600 Bolsheviks, gathering to attack the Americans. Captain Moore, in an immediate feat of arms, ordered all three platoons, with machine gun cover, to attack the Bolos in the clearing. Surprised by the boldness of the Doughboys' action, the Reds fled in fear and the clearing was taken without a casualty.

Shortly after the battle ended, the French Colonials who had retreated the day before came walking up, smiling as if nothing had happened. They had been shamed by their commanding officer into rejoining the fight and spread out to guard the flanks. Happy to see their numbers increased again, the Yanks figured c'est la vie, c'est la guerre and welcomed the poilus home.

Having reached Verst 445, the Allies were closing in on the town of Emtsa, a key railway repair station and upriver from important military operations in Kodish, on the Emtsa River.

The Bolos continued days of heavy artillery barrages (but nothing compared to the Western Front!). By orders of General Ironside, however, the Allies would soon be digging in and preparing for the oncoming snows at this, the furthest position south on the Railroad Front.

My dearest wife,

Beautiful fall weather and another envelope for a love letter. They are strict on our regular letters. I can hardly write a love note except in a green envelope. A fellow sure doesn't want to write about love and private matters and have it gazed over by some sergeant looking for military information.

I haven't received a letter for over a month, so can't answer yours. I love you and the kiddies. How glad I'll be to get back to McGrath and see and hug you all again! It drags on so, sweetheart, day after day, as the winter approaches and the sky gets darker.
I almost get discouraged, but still the time does pass. I hope it will be over soon.

You must always keep the smile going, dear and continue with your good times and don't worry as I am situated fine and dandy and feeling strong. Wish I could tell just what we do, but can't, so just take my word for it that all is well.

Keep smiling dear heart and no worries!

Love and kisses to all,

As ever,

Am

Finishing lunch sitting on the banks of the Dvina in Tulgas, I took advantage of a break in the artillery duels and picked up where I had left off in the Book of Mormon. Surely the wisdom in my church's sacred scriptures might bring me solace during my winter in the wilderness. Turning to, again, the Book of Alma, I read in Chapter 20.

After King Lamoni's resurrection and the establishment of a church among his people he requested to go the land of Nephi, to meet his father. The Lord had other things in mind, however, telling Ammon to go to the land of Middoni, where 3 of his brothers were in prison.

Telling Lamoni that the Lord had said his brothers were in prison in Middoni, and that he needed to go and save them, the king offered to help. Being a friend of the king of Middoni, the king offered to travel with him, and help get his brothers out of prison. The king's horses and chariots were prepared, and they immediately left for MIddoni.

As they travelled on the journey towards Middoni, however, they met Lamoni's father, who was angry as his son had not attended a great feast he had held recently. He was also angry that Lamoni was traveling with Ammon, a Nephite, and son of Moises, who he called a liar.

As Lamoni explained why he missed the feast and was traveling with the Nephite to rescue his brothers, his father ordered him to kill Ammon with a sword and return with him to the land of Ishmael.

Lamoni refused to kill Ammon, however, or to return to Ishmael. He said he would go with Ammon to Middoni to release his brothers, knowing that they were "just men and holy prophets of the true God."

His father, angered by his words, drew his sword to strike his own son. Ammon approached him saying not to slay his son, but "it would be better that he should fall than thee, for behold, he has repented of his sins; but if thou should fall at this time, in thine anger, thy soul could not be saved."

Still, the father raised his sword to kill Ammon, who withstood the attack, and struck the king's arm so that he could no longer use it.

The king realized he was likely to be slain by Ammon and begged for him to spare his life. Ammon replied that he would still kill him, unless he would agree to help his brothers to be freed from prison. The king, fearing for his life, told him he would grant whatever he wished, even if it were half of his kingdom.

Hearing this, Ammon asked that his brothers be cast out of prison, and that Lamoni would retain his kingdom and be allowed to be free to act on his own desires. The king agreed to these terms and invited Ammon and his brothers to come visit his kingdom, when they had been freed, as he was impressed by Ammon's words.

Lamoni and Ammon travelled on to Middoni, and, impressing the king of that land, freed his brothers from prison. They were naked, wounded, had been bound in cords and had suffered greatly. Their efforts previously to preach to "hardened and stiff-necked people" who would not listen to their words, had moved them from one place to another, ending up in Middoni and prison.

But now thanks to Ammon and King Lamoni, they were free.

That night, as I slept in a cabin in the lower village in Tulgas, Moroni and Michael again joined me. Having warned me previously of the attack of the "Red Demons," I expected them to, again, provide a vision into the future. But this time they gave me a little lesson in history, leading to this apocalyptic world war we were part of.

I sat by a campfire in the Russian forest, and Michael and Moroni, with only their bright glow and angelic wings indicating they weren't fellow humans, sat beside me. Michael, as the Archangel, spoke first.

"Ammon, you have been baptized in the fire of battle and have survived in the first battles to drive the Red Demons from North Russia. Throughout the country others from the New World and your allies are driving back the forces fighting for a godless world. In Russia, both the Orthodox church and the Old Believers are threatened by the Bolsheviks and other godless forces creating anarchy and conflict across the continent."

Joining him, Moroni spoke. "Followers of our ancestors' faith, the Jews, too, are being massacred in pogroms by both the Reds and the Whites in the chaos that has broken out in this battle at the end of time. It is up to you, Ammon, like your namesake in the Book of Mormon, to be strong and fight for a world that is safe for the godly."

Finally, gaining the temerity to speak to these otherworldly beings, I asked Moroni what had brought him to this time and place in history.

"You ask the right question at the right time, young man. If you remember, before I gained this angelic body, I, Moroni, was a great leader of our tribe, whose father, Mormon, had led the Nephites in battles against the Lamanites, and spread the word of God in ancient times. After great defeats at the hands of the Lamanites, and the deaths of many of our people, I updated and safeguarded the plates with the history of our God's tribes by burying them on the Hill Cumorah…"

I interrupted, as I had always wondered about Moroni's other role, as an angelic messenger.

"…and then, as an angel, you came down to bring the golden plates to Joseph Smith, to fill in the years after Christ was

resurrected and to show the progress of the chosen people in the New World…"

"Yes, in my angelic state, I arrived to bring the good news to the tribes in America. I had spent many years with the plates given to me by my father, Mormon, completed them and brought them to Joseph Smith."

"While I," Michael introjected, "continued to fight for the people of faith in the Old World. Just like new waves of the faithful like the Mormons in the New World, the Old World had its parallels in Martin Luther breaking with the Roman church in the 1500s and the Old Believers leaving the Russian church in the 1600's. As humankind travels on its spiritual journey, I fly through history fighting for God against the Devil no matter what the era. Even the Moslems, some of God's other people, had been fighting the Tsar and Russian domination long before they joined the White Russians fighting the Bolsheviks."

Overwhelmed with the insights and images in this conversation, I smiled at their glowing countenances, then drifted back into the realm of dreamless sleep.

Chapter 5

"K" is For Kodish for Company K

When we had headed out on barges up the Dvina to face hell at the battle of Tulgas, a smaller group of Yanks, Company K, led by the soon to be legendary Captain Donoghue, had been off on another adventure. When we first massed our forces in Archangel, Donoghue and his men were sent down the railroad on a mission to assist a group of Royal Scots, French infantry and American sailors led by Colonel Hazeldon, who were rumored to be surrounded by Bolos and in danger of destruction on the Emtsa River near the strategic town of Kodish, between the Dvina and the Railway Fronts. As you will remember, the crews of two of the 68ths 18 pounders had taken off towards the village of Seletskoe, above Kodish, to assist the forces there, while we were moving towards Tulgas.

From the Allied base on the railroad at Obozerskaya, Donoghue and his 120 Michigan infantry and medical men marched southeast carrying ammunition, tents, ground covers and rations in horse drawn Russian "droshky" carriages. The muddy road was surrounded by a forest of spruce, pine and birch. Camping that night on the trail in a cold drizzle, they moved on the next day, finding the remnants of a battlefield where Hazeldon's allied force had been in combat with and was badly beaten by the Bolsheviks. Several graves and written material by a British officer and an American sailor told Donoghue they had found the earlier battlefield. The Bolsheviks were numerous in this sector, as they were trying to beat back advances towards Kodish and, especially, Plesetskaya and Emtsa, the supply bases supporting their advances on the Railroad, Vaga and Dvina fronts.

To prepare to reach and cross the Emtsa River and move south towards Kodish, Donoghue's troops first would need to take the village of Seletskoe. Trying to reach the Emtsa River, they hiked for five days, but the wet trails through the swamps were too muddy. Receiving newly trained machine gun reinforcements down from Bakharitsa, Donoghue got orders to continue his advance to Seletskoe. Reaching the village, he found the Bolos had evacuated, letting the villagers know they would soon return. Setting up a perimeter, K Company had barely dug in before the Bolsheviks returned and attacked. Using French machine gun fire effectively, the Yanks held off the Bolos for two days. Finally, having suffered many casualties attacking the Yanks in Seletskoe, the Bolos shot their commander and retreated 30 versts upriver.

In the confusion of the battle along the Emtsa, the Yanks got word that more Bolos were on the way, so they retreated across the river to Tiogra and burned the bridge to Seletskoe, to keep the Bolos from chasing them. Meanwhile, the Bolos, thinking they had been flanked, crossed the Emtsa further upstream, burning a bridge behind them, to keep the Yanks from reaching them.

A British corporal at one of the outposts near Seletskoe, after noticing the Bolos had burned their bridge, returned to Seletskoe, and seeing the yanks digging in on the other side of the bridge they had burned, yelled "I say, old chaps, what's the bloody game?"

By September 23, though, the Yanks had taken back Seletskoe, and, after improving the defenses, received more infantry reinforcements from the Railroad Front, and a Russian and an American machine gun platoon. With Seletskoe secure, Gen. Finlayson ordered the Yanks to move south to take Kodish, as the next step in reaching the Bolshevik supply base at Plesetskaya, and perhaps moving on to Emtsa. So on September 26, K and L companies headed south with one machine gun company, towards Kodish.

They caught up with the Bolsheviks near where they had crossed and burned the bridge on the Emtsa River. The Bolos were dug in well on the other side of the river, so the Americans sent a landing party across by raft. Attacking the Reds, they suffered severe casualties. Lt Chappel led a group attacking a Bolo machine gun position and was mortally wounded. Soon the Yanks dug in, but by the time they reached a stalemate, six other Allies were killed, and 24 wounded. Droshkys were kept busy driving back and forth to Seletskoe carrying the allied casualties.

It was clear reinforcements would be needed to continue the advance to Kodish. At this point, our Canadian lads from the 68th Artillery Battalion arrived with the much needed 18 pounders to knock some sense into the Bolos across the river. A force of English Marines also arrived, and a headquarters was set up in the tiny village of Mejnovsky, eight miles down the river.

A new British officer, Lt. Gavin, arrived on Oct 7, with a bold plan to advance on the Bolos across the river. 3 versts south of Mejnovsky, he had the 310 Yank Engineers build a ferry across the river. By Oct 12, Companies K and L had all crossed the river and advanced towards within 1000 yards of the Bolshevik position and camped in the swamp for the night. The next day Captain Cherry with Company L and 2 platoons of Company K, flanked the Bolo forces concentrated along the river, heading towards the town of Kodish itself. In the meantime, firing from the British Marines, American machine guns and the Canadian 18 pounders across the river kept the Bolshevik's attention faced in their direction. Due to the depth and breadth of the swamps they faced, Captain Cherry's force failed to reach its objective behind the Reds. In the meantime, Donoghue had to dig in and repulse 2 Bolshevik counterattacks and suffered severe casualties trying to take 2 Bolo machine gun nests.

The next day L Company and the British marines, having crossed the river during the night, began to advance and make progress against the Bolos in the woods. The Reds counterattacked, however, and the Allies spent another miserable night sleeping in the swamps. Perhaps good and angry after another night in the woods, they arose the next morning and attacked towards the village of Kodish, pushing the Bolsheviks into a retreat down the road to Plesetskaya. Donoghue set up his headquarters in the now allied controlled village of Kodish and sent detachments to chase after the retreating Reds.

Following the fighting in Kodish, some of our Canadian lads came into town and taught the green Yanks the correct etiquette of robbing the dead. Being new to combat, the Yanks were shy about rifling through the pockets of the recently deceased, but our boys, after 4 years in the trenches in France, assured them it would be waste to ignore the resources of the many Bolos killed here. They checked their pockets for rubles, pocketknives or other treasures and often would find a decent pair of military boots or Russian valenkis, warn felt peasant boots. These were popular as our military issue and Shackleton boots were, as previously noted, no great shakes. But most of the lads didn't bother with the Russian tobacco which was even worse than that of English cigarettes. They would always prefer the Yanks' smokes, provided, of course, by the YMCA.

Excited that they had driven the Bolos from Kodish, many of the troops were ready to charge ahead and fight their way to Plesetskaya. The Bolshevik command and Trotsky himself, however, were determined to hold that key base. So initially, the advances past Kodish were repeatedly blocked by Soviet forces just 15 versts out of town.

Before they could proceed much further, though, word came from General Ironside that, with winter coming on, all units needed to "hold on and dig in". The treacherous Arctic freeze was setting in, and neither we, nor the Bolsheviks, would be in a position to make much progress before Spring. Digging in and consolidating our gains was the best we could do. This meant, to strengthen our various positions, we would be moving troops around to make sure all our fronts were adequately defended.

For the Canadians, this meant the 68th Battalion Artillery headed back to the Dvina Front and L Company and the British Marines were withdrawn from Kodish. Reduced to 180 Americans, Donoghue's force to defend Kodish was inadequate, at best. He placed a 4-man crew in an outpost at 17 versts. At the 16 verst pole he placed 2 machine guns, a Lewis Gun and 46 men. 4 miles behind this, in the old Bolo dugouts, were 40 men and a Vickers gun. A mile behind was the village of Kodish itself, with the balance of Company K, both active and wounded, and 4 Vickers guns.

On November 1st, the Bolsheviks attacked the Verst 17 outpost, pouring rifle and artillery fire into the position. By the 4th of November, despite brave resistance by the Yanks, the Reds drove through to capture the Verst 16 position. Then by the 5th, Bolo fire could be heard from the other side of the village, indicating Company K was completely surrounded.

Despite their desperate position, they kept fighting for days. By the 8th, even threatened by Bolos on the bridge that was their only escape from Kodish, they fought on.

Suddenly, Colonel Hazelden, whose force was wiped out earlier in the area, arrived in the midst of the fight to defend Kodish. As he took command, fresh Bolshevik troops from South Russia also arrived, sent by Trotsky to strengthen his Northern Army, and were pouring into the battle. Joining the 40 Americans in the 12th Verst dugouts, Hazelden witnessed the Yanks' Lewis and Vickers guns mowing down the fresh Russian troops. Breaking and running for the woods, the screams of fear and the cries of the wounded Bolos led Donoghue to fear that his own troops were getting the worst of it. Yet, the American's survived and held out through the night. Digging in across the bridge, Company K began building blockhouses, laying barbed wire and trenching as they followed Ironside's orders to "dig in and hold on" through the winter. Hazeldon returned to headquarters, relief troops and artillery were on their way to Kodish, and Company K moved back to reserve status in Seletskoe. Then, finally, they marched to Obozerskaya and took a train trip to Archangel for a much needed and well-earned rest.

Reflecting on the casualties experienced by the Yanks in and around Kodish, Abe later commented on the coincidence of the town's name, Kodish, sometimes spelled Kadish, being so similar to Kaddish, the Jewish prayer for the dead. I asked him what the words of the Kaddish prayer were. He translated into English, first the words of the Rabbi: "Exalted and sanctified be his great name, in the world which he created according to His will! May he establish His kingdom and may His salvation blossom and his anointed be near during your lifetime and during your days and during the lifetimes of all the House of Israel, speedily and very soon! And say Amen." He then translated the words of the congregation: "May His great name be blessed forever, and to all eternity! Blessed and praised, glorified and exalted, extolled and honored, adored and lauded, be the name of the Holy One, blessed be He, above and beyond all the blessings, hymns, praises and consolations that are uttered in the world! And say, Amen."

And say Amen, we did, for those who survived, and those who died, during the bloody fights in Kodish.

Another experience the 339th lads had on the Kodish front illustrated the ongoing propaganda the Bolos were throwing at us all over the Archangel province. Not only were trainloads of leaflets in English, French and other languages posted here there and everywhere throughout the area, we also often heard from trained orators speaking to us from the darkness of the forests.

In late January on the Kodish front, a Bolshevik propagandist, with a voice the boys described as "ghostlike" and having a "New York accent", began speaking to them from the woods. "Americans, can you hear me?" he called out.

To avoid getting shot, the doughboys at first stayed silent. The orator tried again twice, with "Can you hear me?"

Eager for the chance to shoot it out with him, one of the Yanks yelled "Where the hell are you?"

Assured he had an audience, the Bolo began his speech, which echoed through the forest silence.

"Why are you fighting us, Americans? We are your brothers! We are all working men. You American boys are shedding your blood up here in Russia, and I ask you, for what reason? My friends and comrades, you should be back home. The war with Germany is over and you have no war with us. The co-workers of the world are uniting in opposition to capitalism. Why are you being kept here? Can you answer that question? No! We don't want to fight you, as you are our brothers. But we do want to fight the capitalists, and your officers are capitalists!"

He went on for 20 minutes like this, then must have headed deeper into the forest.

This was the kind of message we heard, repeatedly, throughout the winter of 1918-1919. If the Bolos didn't recruit any converts to their new religion, it was surely not for lack of trying!

My dearest wife,

Everything still going fine and dandy, though the winter is surely coming on. We eat and sleep like horses out here in the forest villages. Horses like the little Russian ponies they call horses which we care for much of our time so they can haul our guns.

We often are billeted in sheds or barns of the local villagers, or in their cabins. The whole house in Russia is built around a big brick stove. It is so big some of the folks actually sleep up on it. Lots of animals and animal dung in close quarters in the houses, so you have to get used to plenty of smells.

Everywhere we go, of course, we get crumby with lice. They clean us up once in a great while, but we stay dirty and crumby all the time.

But you bet, dear, I will get cleaned up before we start our honeymoon when I return! When we meet again, be sure and bring a clean pair of garments, and I will wear my freshest uniform. Your loyal Ammon will love you like you have never been loved before.

So, cheer up and don't be blue at all. I feel completely healed from my blighty wound back in France, and plan to stay safe and healthy for my return to you.

This experience, and the test of the Great War, has made a much more responsible man of me, and I believe you will be proud of the new man I am when I get home.

I love you dear and will be so glad to get back, have good times and never will I leave you again. Have dreamed about the kiddies the past two nights, especially Luana. Hope she has not been sick. Bless their dear little hearts and bless yours, sweetheart. Keep smiling!

With Love,

Am

Returning to my reading, I moved over to the Book of Mosiah to learn more about Ammon's travels and battles. Starting in Chapter 11, I found more conflict between the Nephites and the Lamanites, and a scene reminiscent of the plates Joseph Smith found in New York state, on a hill called Cumorah, inspiring the Mormon church.

After Limhi and his people returned to the city of Nephi in about 122 B.C. they were living at peace. But the Lamanites, again, began stirring up trouble on the borders of their land. Having agreed with Limhi not to kill his people, they still beat them, enslaved them and treated them like animals of burden.

Finally, the Nephites rose up, donned their armor and attacked the Lamanites to drive them out of their land. At first, many of the Nephites were killed and driven back. The rest of the people of Lemhi, angered by this defeat, went into battle again, and again were defeated. Trying a third time, they were again beaten back to the city of Nephi and served as workers and servants of the Lamanites.

Praying to God, they were gradually heard, and began improving their crops, their flocks and their herds. The widows of those slain in the wars were cared for. The king had the people guard the city more carefully.

As peace returned to the people of Limhi, Ammon and his brothers returned to the land. Mistaking them for the evil priests of Noah, Limhi had them bound and put into prison. Finding they were not Noah's priests, Limhi released them, and realizing they were his brethren from the land of Zarahemla, he was happy they were home.

Before Ammon arrived, the king had sent a group to find the land of Zarahemla but had not found it. They did, however, find a once populated area, which was covered with dry bones that had been destroyed. The expedition, assuming this to be Zarahemla, brought records of the people whose bones they found, engraved on plates of ore.

Ammon explained that king Mosiah, his father, had a gift from God, and could translate these kinds of engravings, which filled both Limni and Ammon with joy. Ammon and his brothers, however, were sad to hear how many brethren had been slain in the battles with the Lamanites.

They also learned that king Noah and his priests had caused people to sin against God and that Alma and others who had formed a church of God had departed, and no one knew where they fled.

Ammon and his brethren, who had entered into a covenant with God, would have liked to join with them. King Limhi, also entered into a covenant with many of his people to serve God and keep his commandments.

Ammon was asked by Limhi to baptize him and many of his people but Ammon did not consider himself a worthy servant of God and did not baptize them. They were all hoping to be baptized and become servants of God.

So they studied on how Ammon and his people and Limhi and his people, could free themselves of bondage by the Lamanites.

Chapter 6

Digging in for the Winter

As November turned into December, winter descended on the Archangel Province. From the north, where even icebreakers could no longer cross the White Sea to bring supplies, to the rivers iced over so that neither Bolo nor English gunboats could operate, we were beginning to dig in for the winter on the 5 fingers of the Archangel front. As days began dropping to well below zero, all the heavy coats, Shackleton Boots and skis came out, and our artillery and gear began to be dragged on sleighs with reindeers or ponies along snow covered forest paths and frozen rivers.

While the bulk of the 67th remained in the area around Tulgas, the 68th had moved into the city of Shenkursk, further south on the Vaga River. A small contingent of the 67th however, had originally been sent from Archangel down to another finger of the front, south of Obozerskaya, an allied base on the railroad to Moscow. This contingent consisted of 3 officers, 20 gunners and 3 signalmen assigned to an armored train on the Railroad Front. Originally some Royal Marines had captured this armored train, and the 68th boys helped run communications and arm the train to fight the Bolos. Their train had two flatcars ahead of the engine, with sandbags surrounding a machine gun on one and a machine gun and an 18 pounder on the other. Behind the armored engine was a car with two large naval guns and another machine gun. Following were sleeping and eating cars for the troops. 2 other trains were run by Polish, British and White Russian troops. These travelling fortresses, both on the allied and the Bolshevik side, did a lot of the fighting on the railroad front. Other infantry and artillery, of course, working in blockhouses and trenches, made up the rest of the frontlines, and spent a lot of time killing each other and either blowing up track or repairing it.

As the Bolsheviks and the Allies dug in with blockhouses and log cabins as well as trenches and barbed wire along the railroad, they created the fairly permanent zone, about 300 Versts south of Archangel, that became, for the winter, the frontline of this finger.

When I briefly visited the guys on the railroad front, they had even set up a cinema in the HQ of one of the railroad front trains. One night we watched one of our most famous Canadians, Mary Pickford, and thought of our wives, children, friends and lovers back home. But soon my comrades from the 67th were sent back to the Dvina front, and I was transferred to the 68th, now short on drivers, in the beautiful city of Shenkursk.

The several thousand residents of Shenkursk, a resort town before the war, and established originally by Catherine The Great, had no love for the Bolsheviks or the revolution. Shenkursk was the 2nd largest town in the Archangel district. It was a city of comfortable houses, businesses, schools, lumber mills and a large monastery which welcomed the allies with open arms. Actually, when the British and the Americans originally came to Beresnik to plan their advance up the Dvina and the Vaga, a group of Shenkursk residents travelled there and met with them, asking them to defend their city against the Red Army, gathering to the south in Vologda.

So when Americans Captain Odjard and Lt Mead, with a platoon of Company A, travelled in a steamer with a gunboat to Shenkursk in September, they were welcomed with open arms. The Bolos, after looting part of the town, hightailed it south without firing a shot.

With many beautiful multistoried homes and office buildings there, Odjard and Mead had no trouble finding a site for the U.S. headquarters. The British, however, as usual, came in and let the Yanks know their job was to move upriver and engage the Bolos, while the British would set up the base in

Shenkursk. They did, however, allow the U.S. 337 Field Hospital to set up in a converted 2 story school building, anticipating casualties as the Bolsheviks moved up from Vologda in force.

Before all hell broke loose in Shenkursk, General Ironside had visited the city to check out the situation. His Russian speaking groom Piskoff had heard from locals about their desire to rid the region of the Allied troops and that a large attack was imminent on Shenkursk. If it was surrounded, it would be difficult, as far south as it was, to send reinforcements from Archangel. Should the Allies retreat from the city? On one hand, the Allies had substantial forces in and south of the city. 400 local recruits had been trained and were enthusiastic and ready to fight. To pull back from the city now would discourage them and put the townspeople at risk.

In his memoirs, Ironside admitted he was tempted to stay in Shenkursk, take command and assist in the fight to defend it. With his responsibilities as commander of the whole region, however, he realized that wasn't practical. He left orders to mount a robust defense but to evacuate the city if necessary.

Later, when travelling home from Archangel with the Canadian forces, I spoke with Piskoff, who pointed out how Ironside had showed his dedication and grit as a general by not only travelling from one front to another, but doing so without accompanying troops. With his driver, Kostia, a 16-year-old Russian who had volunteered to work for him, and Piskoff, he moved from front to front by sleigh for hundreds of miles along narrow forest trails.

Only once, after visiting Shenkursk, and on his way to the Dvina front in January, did he encounter hostile forces. With Piskoff and Kostia in a sleigh in front, Ironside was bundled up in a sleeping bag in the second sleigh, hoping to get to his destination soon. He suddenly heard a shout and a shot and his driver stopped, throwing himself to the snow on the ground while holding the horse's reins. Several more shots rang out and bullets were swishing through the bushes behind them. PIskoff and Kostia fired multiple rounds with their automatics. Ironside tumbled into the snow, and, grabbing a rifle from his sleigh, joined PIskoff and Kostia. They saw more flashes of enemy fire 20 yards off and fired a few more rounds. Then they heard a man shout and a pony scream in pain. The three of them walked forward and found an overturned sleigh and a wounded pony. Behind them was a wounded Bolo. There was a lot of blood on the sleigh and on the snow around it.

They the Bolo up and gave him a shot of rum, but he was badly wounded. Piskoff questioned him in Russian. He said that he was on his way to Archangel to set up a propaganda base there. The other sleigh in his party belonged to a Commissar who had gotten away. Piskoff asked who his contacts were on his mission, but he died before he could answer.

They loaded the body, killed by two automatic shots to the chest, aboard the front sleigh with Piskoff and Kostia joined Ironside on the second sleigh. Unable to find any paper or other evidence on the Bolo or on his sled, they headed on to their destination.

As my friend Abe proved that his rudimentary Russian was enough to communicate with the residents of the region, he had been transferred to the Yanks' Company A moving up the Vaga, so he and I reunited south of Shenkursk due to my posting there with Hydes' 68th Artillery Battalion. But before we connected, he had some adventures with Odjard and Mead chasing the Bolos on a steamer called the *Tolstoy*. Near a village called Goka they were fired on and pursued by the enemy through swamps and a forest without overcoats and short on rations. They reached the furthest point south of any of the allied troops at a village called Puya. There they encountered a large force of Bolos and got caught in a crossfire between them and another group behind them.

They fought bravely, killing 50 of the enemy and suffering only 4 wounded. From this position, seeing the strength of the Bolshevik forces in the area, they retreated. By mid-October they were joined by more of the 310th Engineers and began building a defensive line of log blockhouses, dugouts and barbed wire entanglements in the villages of Ust Padenga and Nijni Gora, 15 miles south of Shenkhursk.

As this was our last line of defense below the city of Shenkursk, I was stationed with the 68th and several of our guns were close enough to where Abe was billeted in Ust Padenga that we shared a few meals and drinks, as the winter set in. Our unit traded off with some Cossack White Russian artillerymen on these guns, at which time we would get days off back in Shenkhursk.

On one of these opportunities for respite behind the lines, a number of us from the 68th joined Abe and the boys from Company A at a Thanksgiving dinner put on in the big hospital building in Shenkursk. Probably, along with a Christmas dinner we had later there and eating at the Café de Paris, among the best meals we ever ate in North Russia. Also, due to Shenkursk being a more aristocratic, prosperous and educated city, the local girls invited to the events were not the usual peasant barishnas, but were bright, charmingly dressed and, to these lonely soldiers, beautiful. With a band consisting of a violin, a guitar and a banjo, we sang seasonal songs and laughed as one of the boys improvised a song about the cooties (lice) to the tune of "Over There." "The bugs are crawling, the bugs are crawling, the bugs are crawling, everywhere!"

It was at this dance that I met one of the most amazing women I had encountered in my life. Amy Selma Valentine, or Nurse Valentine as she was known, was part Russian and part British and spoke a number of languages. She had lived

76

in St Petersburg, studying at the Smolny Institute, and, during the revolution, heard the speeches of Lenin and Trotsky. During the "Red Terror" after an assassination attempt against Lenin, she was suspected of being too friendly with the British and was detained. Later she escaped and joined the British forces in Archangel as an interpreter. Moving to Shenkursk, she began helping as a nurse during the Spanish flu epidemic. When the Allies took over the city, she continued as a nurse for their soldiers.

That night I came the closest to being unfaithful to my dear Florence, as I shared some rum in hot tea, of all things, with Nurse Valentine. As we found a quiet corner of the hospital, and talked of our lives and our dreams, a wave of affection came over me that I couldn't control. Putting my loyalty to Fife and the three kids aside, I allowed myself to throw my arms around Nurse Valentine and kiss her, like I had never kissed anyone before. I felt both animal passion and as if, for the first time in my life, I was truly in love.

Pulling myself together, I thought about my promises to Fife and pulled away. I apologized for being too forward and walked her back to the dance. I hoped that she would forgive me, but I also hoped to see her again before this strange adventure in North Russia came to an end.

Little did Abe and I know that our chance for romance and relaxation in Shenkursk at Thanksgiving may have saved our lives. For, while we were carousing with beautiful women and enjoying a little rum, our replacements in Ust Padenga from Company C were about to face a disaster.

Before we returned, on November 29th, Lt Cuff took 100 men to attack a strong position of Bolos in the area. They marched through deep snow and the weather had dipped to 20 below zero. As they neared the Vaga on a narrow forest trail, they were assaulted by an even larger Bolshevik force.

Rifle fire rang throughout the forest as most of Cuff's platoon retreated towards Ust Padenga. A small group, however, was surrounded near the river. Cuff returned to help with a handful of men, but they were also surrounded. With Cuff mortally wounded, in a scene reminiscent of the Battle of Little Big horn, he and his men were wiped out.

When their bodies were recovered and returned to Shenkursk, we were witnesses to them having been not only killed but mutilated by the Bolos. At their funeral Capt Kinyon made a speech noting the Bolos had castrated some of our boys when they were still alive and that Lt Cuff had grabbed his revolver and shot himself. "That is the kind of enemy we are fighting," Kinyon finished. He also noted that Cuff and his brave troops had left a circle of dead Bolsheviks around them, indicating the intensity of the battle.

The parade of troops carrying their bodies to graves at the edge of the forest was an impressive international gathering including British and American troops, White Russian infantry, the Royal Scots in their bonnets and bagpipes, our Canadian Artillery unit and mounted Cossack Cavalry in their tall hats and bandoleers. But this would be far from the last funeral parade we would see in North Russia.

As the snow got deeper, and the winter got colder, we began to realize how precarious our situation was on the Vaga River front. Our position in Shenkursk and the surrounding villages was 50 miles further south than Tulgas on the Dvina and 80 miles below Verst 445 on the Railroad Front. As the Red Army continued to strengthen its forces in our area, they could not only attack us from the South, but from the East and West as well. It was clear it was only a matter of time before the Bolos would attack in force to drive us out of our forward positions and Shenkursk.

A small group of the Yanks' 339th, including my friend Abe, as well as some Cossack troops, were defending the point furthest south in our intervention in North Russia. They were on a high bluff above the tiny villages of Ust Padenga and

Nijni Gora, below Shenkursk, between the forest and the Vaga River. Our artillery position was nearby, and we alternated shifts on the guns with the group of White Russian gunners.

At dawn on Jan 18, Lt Mead and 44 yanks were suddenly heavily bombarded by Bolshevik artillery from the deep forest across the Vaga. The Bolo gunners were positioned well beyond the range our guns, on that morning manned by the Cossacks. As the barrage continued, the Cossacks deserted their guns. Frustrated to see their gunners retreating, Abe, Mead and the Yanks looked out to see, 1500 yards across the snow, hundreds of Bolos charging towards them in dark uniforms. Slowing them down with rifle fire, they then saw, as the Bolo artillery finally stilled, hundreds of more Reds, dressed all in white, charging out of snow filled ravines surrounding them. With a virtual handful of defenders, the yanks kept pouring rifle and machine gun fire at the attackers.

Corporal Stier, seeing one of the Cossacks had abandoned his machine gun, ran up and continued a deadly fire at the Bolos. Hit in the jaw by a bullet, he continued to fight until ordered back to the village. On his way through, he picked up a rifle, dropped by a dead comrade, and kept firing, determined to fight to the very end. Wounded again, mortally, he fought till falling unconscious, and died later that day.

Meanwhile, with our artillery stilled by the desertion of the Cossacks, Captain Odjard rounded them up at pistol point and forced them back to their guns. This was too late to be of any help to the Yanks, however, as the circle of white clad Bolsheviks closed in. The small group of Yanks continued firing at the charging Bolos, though they were being peppered with rifle and automatic fire. Gradually the front line of Yanks fell back to the rear and all fought house to house through the village, retreating from the Reds.

Finally convinced by Lt Odyard to do their jobs, the Cossack gunners loaded and fired shrapnel at some of the 900 Bolsheviks now surrounding them, giving the Yanks time to retreat and prepare a run for the main body of their troops. By this time, at 45 degrees below zero and wading through waist deep snow, the troops were almost wiped out as they struggled down a hillside and across an open field in an 800 yard "valley of death." In a platoon of 47 men, 7 made it across the field to shelter. Abe joined a rescue party from Company A, headed by Lt McPhail, which braved continuing enemy fire to save as many of the wounded as possible, but most had died of their wounds or had frozen solid in snowy graves.

By nightfall the Cossacks in Ust Padenga, the surviving Yanks and we Canadians prepared our defenses nearer to Nijni Gora. The faraway Bolo guns kept pounding us with artillery fire and, by morning, long lines of Bolo infantry were again on the attack. Confused, though, they charged at the recently evacuated Ust Padenga. Taking advantage of this, we fired at a distance at the charging Bolos. With our Canadian gunners back on the artillery, we took a lesson from the battle of Tulgas, loaded the cannons with shrapnel, and cut down dozens more of the Soviet troops. The snowy field was soon littered with bloody enemy bodies.

Seeing he was taking far too many casualties, the Bolo commander halted the infantry charge and pivoted to delivering the worst artillery barrage we had yet experienced. Soon thousands of shells were pounding us while we could not even attempt to reach the Bolo guns across the river. Towards the end of the day, a shell hit the village hospital where medical office Ralph Powers was operating on one of the wounded. Four in the hospital were killed in the blast and Powers was mortally wounded. He died later in Shenkursk, and was buried with more of our brave lads, near the cathedral.

By January 22 it was clear that the Bolshevik forces were gathering for an assault on Shenkursk itself. By orders of the British command, all allied troops began retreating towards Shenkursk. One of our 18 pounders, which our tired Russian ponies couldn't pull through the snow, had to be spiked and was left behind on the trail. Shells burst behind us as we retreated, leaving Ust Padenga in flames. The homes and lives of more Russian peasants were being destroyed by the rapidly growing conflagration between the Whites and the Reds in Archangel province.

With almost nothing to eat, we struggled for two nights hiking through the frozen forest trails to the town of Spasskoe, 6 versts south of Shenkursk. On the way we learned the Bolos had already got ahead of us, taking villages on both sides of the river. But, with the Vaga frozen solid, we took a gamble and headed right up the river between the enemy held villages. Travelling at night and hoping any noise we made would be thought to be their comrades on the other side of the river, we succeeded in getting safely to Spasskoe. We hoped to take a brief rest there, and have some hard tack and bully beef, but that wasn't in the cards.

Climbing into a church tower, Lt Mead and Captain Mowat, our artillery commander, could see lines of Bolshevik artillery pieces heading up the road towards Shenkursk, with hundreds of Bolo troops gathering in nearby villages. We quickly formed skirmish lines, and soon were taking artillery fire from units that were already bombarding Shenkursk. By midday a shell hit our last 18 pounder, putting it out of action. The shell killed several men and seriously wounded Capt Odjard and Captain Mowatt, who died later of their wounds.

We got on the telephone with Shenkursk and were ordered to continue our retreat just before a shell burst and ended our communications. Skirting the Bolo forces, we found our way to the city, hungry and exhausted, by evening.

My Sweetheart Wife,

We have moved and have seen more action since I last wrote. I am stationed near my friend Abe, who I told you about in my

81

letter from Archangel. He and the yanks have seen a lot of action, and some heavy casualties. As usual, dear, in our artillery unit, we are stationed behind the front line, and we have had only a few of our boys hurt. I am doing fine.

For Thanksgiving we got a break and enjoyed a dinner at the hospital in a real city with schools, lumber mills and educated citizens—not just the villagers in the forests. We had great food and fun. I met a nurse who is part Russian and part British and speaks a bunch of languages. Her name is Selma Valentine, and I'm sure you would like her.

Don't worry though, love, as my only Valentine and true love is you, dear, and I would never think of anyone else. I showed her a picture of you and the little ones, and she was very impressed.

Keep smiling, dear, and have the good times. I'm fine and dandy and there is nothing to worry about. But I'll be glad when I get back and show you by my actions that all I've told you is true. I know you'll believe me until then.

With love, yours always.

Am

Before dozing off on the floor of the Shenkursk barracks, I picked up my Book of Mormon, reading what seemed like an appropriate chapter for our current situation, facing the need for a retreat from Shenkursk. It was Chapter 22 of Mosiah, describing the escape from a city and returning to Zarahemla.

Ammon and King Limhi sought the people's opinions on how they could deliver themselves from bondage. They agreed that to get out of bondage, they would need to take their women, their children, their flocks, their herds and their possessions and depart into the wilderness. Because the Lamanites were

*so numerous, they felt it was impossible to do battle with
them.*

*On behalf of the people, Gideon proposed to the king that the
people gather their herds and possessions and prepare, at a
back pass, in the back wall of the city, to drive them into the
wilderness at night. The Lamanites, often drunken in the night,
would likely not catch them, if they left through this secret
pass.*

*Leaving with their people, their flocks and their herds into the
wilderness, they would travel through the land of Shilom. And
Ammon and his brethren led them around Shilom on the way
to Zarahemla.*

*They took with them their gold and silver and valuable
possessions which they could, and their provisions, and
travelled to the land of Zarahemla and joined Mosiah's people
and became his subjects. Mosiah received them with joy and
received the records that had been found by the people of
Limhi.*

*The Lamanites, finding the people of Limhi had left, sent
troops to follow them in the wilderness, following for two days,
but lost their track, and spent time lost in the wilderness.*

My angelic visitor that night was just the Angel Moroni. He had
come to give me solace in our time of danger. Just like the
ancient tribes of Israel, in their escape from bondage, or the
Mormons of the 19th Century, in their journey from Nauvoo to
the Great Salt Lake, we would need God's guidance and
protection in our epic escape from Shenkursk.

*Appearing again as the golden angelic figure, as if atop a
Mormon temple, Moroni blew his horn, and cried out, "Ammon,
have no fear! The Lord is with you in meeting the dangers you
face. Have faith, as he will be guiding you through the*

wilderness."

In those simple words, he set my mind at rest, and I dissolved into a sea of light. Peace was with me.

Chapter 7

The Siege of Shenkursk

As we slept in the barracks in Shenkursk, British command was weighing our options. We had enough food, supplies, guns and ammunition to hold out in this city for perhaps 60 days. The Bolsheviks, however, had already surrounded Shenkursk and were pounding us with artillery. In the dead of winter, the chances of bringing more troops down from Archangel to relieve us or of breaking through the growing ring of Bolos surrounding us, was close to nil. With the Dvina and Vaga frozen over, we would not get help from Allied gunboats for at least 4 months. On the other hand, even if we could retreat, it was over 100 miles to our base at Beresnik,

Learning that there was one forest trail that the enemy hadn't noticed, mounted Cossacks rode out to assess the possibility of a nocturnal retreat. They returned saying that, due to the deep snow, the Bolos had not occupied this path. We decided it could handle the mounted Cossacks, our artillery, the infantry, refugees from Shenkursk and sleighs loaded with the wounded from the hospital. It wound through the forest north and would take us to the next town up the river, Shegovari.

Just before the telephone lines to headquarters in Beresnik were cut, British command there ordered us to evacuate the city. We requisitioned every pony sleigh and driver in the city, preparing for our retreat. All was going well when the British announced that, due to the danger in the journey and the need for speed, we would have to leave the wounded behind in the hospital. This, or course, didn't sit well with we Canadians and the Yanks, and after an angry confrontation, it was decided they, too, would be loaded onto the sleighs. When I discovered that Nurse Valentine would be accompanying the wounded in our retreat from Shenkursk, I personally became more invested in the conversation. Ordered to pack lightly, many of the lads were grabbing anything they could eat and throwing out anything they didn't need to survive. Rather than destroying any ammunition and equipment we couldn't carry, which would alert the Bolos to our retreat, we had to leave it behind to be captured.

At 0100 hours, with the Aurora Borealis writhing like a dragon to our north, and the Cossack cavalry taking the lead, we in the artillery began moving up the trail. We passed between the barbed wire entanglements and the blockhouses on the north edge of town. Behind us were over 50 sleighs carrying 100 sick and wounded. They were loaded in pairs in each sled, lined with straw, and given a shot of medicine or rum before starting on their journey, tended by Nurse Valentine and the Yanks of the 337 Field Hospital unit. Following the sleighs were over 1,000 infantrymen from all units, and over 5,000 residents, some leaving their homes for the first, and probably, the last time. The Russian men, women and children walking by their sleighs loaded with as many of their possessions as they could carry were a tragic sight. Even some of the comely young barishnas we had met at Thanksgiving were among the refugees, but I could only think about Nurse Valentine, of course.

Some of the local Russians in the Shenkursk Battalion, who we had recruited and trained, were sent out on another trail to cover our retreat if the Bolos discovered us. We were worried that some with Bolshevik sympathies might not be loyal when the fighting started. Our fears were justified, it seems, when, encountering a Bolo unit, after trading a few shots, most of these troops surrendered and went over to the other side. A few retreated back towards Shenkursk. But this would be far from the last time our White Russian allies shifted their allegiance to the Reds.

Bringing up the rear behind the residents were the dog-tired men of Company A. They had been in combat for nearly a week with little sleep or food. They stumbled in the deep snow, rutted by hundreds of sleighs ahead of them. Their Shackleton boots, designed by the famous arctic explorer, were worth the powder to blow them to hell, they learned, as their slick surfaces slipped in the snow. Snow which was rutted with sleigh tracks and the pockmarks of hundreds of boots and horses' hooves. Some wag later wrote a brief poem on the odd gait created by walking in the Shackleton boot: "One step forward and two steps back- a sideslip down with a hell of a whack!"

Later, as the column inched its way through the darkness and 35 degrees below zero cold, ice laden spruce limbs broke and fell on the trail, with loud cracks. Occasionally one of the Russian sleighs would overturn, sending the family's possessions onto the snowbank. The family would grab what they could, reload the sleigh and move on. After what seemed like forever, we left the tunnel of the forest heading downhill into a clearing on the frozen Vaga. Then, crossing the river, we headed back into the darkness of the forest.

As a gray dawn approached, the Bolshevik artillery, including heavier 7 and 9 inch guns and several howitzers, began raining an apocalyptic barrage of shells behind us on Shenkursk, now ten miles away. Relieved as this indicated they were unaware of our retreat, we picked up our pace to further distance ourselves from the enemy.

An hour later, in full daylight, our line spread out through a long village called Yemska Gora. Accommodating villagers offered tea from their samovars and allowed us to thaw out our canteens and cans of corned beef and frozen hardtack. Some of the Shenkursk refugees used the stop to move up in the column, to get a safer position in the retreat. The Russian villagers' hospitality, in sharing space around their big brick stoves, thawed out the hearts and bodies of our travelers, before we started up again towards Shegovari.

After an hour, in the middle of the day, with the wind diminished, we set out again. In a few hours we passed a group of windmills, reminding me of the giants an old knight fought on the hillsides of Spain in Don Quixote. Then, rising gradually to a higher elevation, we looked out at the vast panorama before us, with the column winding for miles on its journey through the forests to safety.

Before sunset, we finally reached the village of Shegovari, 20 miles due north of Shenkursk. The Vaga makes several looping turns here, like a person's intestines, before heading north towards Beresnik. As we entered the village, the garrison of Yanks from Company C and D came out to greet us. They told us that the Bolos, dressed as peasants, had been raiding the village for several days. 200 of them attacked the day before, but the small garrison of Yanks were able to drive them off.

Finding some time for rest in the village, Nurse Valentine and the boys from the 337th Hospital Company began moving the wounded into a large barn that was being used as a barracks. All the ill and wounded had survived except a school master from Shenkursk who died quietly on the trail. After feeding and making all their patients comfortable, and having been awake for over 30 hours, the hospital staff and others of the Yanks lay down in the barn's alfalfa hay without removing even coats or Shackleton boots. They slept the sleep of the dead till late the next day.

I, of course, couldn't ignore Nurse Valentine's presence in our party and hiked over to find her to share a romantic interlude looking out over the icy Vaga and sharing some of my hard tack and bully beef. A self-confidant and fearless young lady, she seemed not at all fazed by this exhausting and dangerous journey. We chatted, expressed our intention of connecting again when we reached the next opportunity and returned to our billets.

Breakfasting on more hard tack, bully beef and tea, we gunners lounged around the barn for the rest of the day. Some enterprising souls among our farriers, tired of slipping and sliding in the Shackleton boots, found some hammers and nails, and began fastening cleats to their boot bottoms. A bunch of the dough boys followed suit, to try and make travelling on the icy Russian trails less treacherous.

Having rested up, the column began forming for the next leg of our journey. We could hear machine gun fire somewhere around the village perimeter and began heading down a steep trail from the village towards the Vaga. To avoid having the sleighs slide in the snow while moving down the incline, a pair of medics would accompany each sleigh and lie down on each side, grasping the sleigh, like human anchors. When they reached the bottom, each pair would run back up the hill to join the next unaccompanied sleigh.

This was a complicated operation, so it was dark when all the patients were down the hill, and the infantry and refugees followed, with the Cossack cavalry riding behind. Soon the long line was passing again into and threading through a tunnel of snow-covered evergreens. Travelling again at night, we soon saw that Shegovari, and the supplies we were forced to leave there, were a red glow in the sky, as the Cossacks had set them afire when they left. On the way towards the town of Kitsa, we saw no villages. Then we reached Vistafka, another Russian town we wouldn't forget. We had decided to make a stand there, four miles before Kitsa, itself 20 miles from Shegovari.

Vistafka was on a high, thickly forested bluff on the right bank of the river, in another set of the Vaga's snake-like loops. While the infantry laid barbed wire and dug snow trenches (the ground was frozen too solid to dig in), the refugees, the wounded and the rest of the column pushed on past us towards Kitsa. Company A and C dug in, covered again by our Canadian guns, making Vistafka the first line of defense for Kitsa. We hung on there, despite repeated Bolo attacks, through February. In early March, with increased artillery and 4,000 troops, the Reds struck Vistafka killing a number of the Yanks. On March 9 we fell back to within 3 versts of Kitsa, a heck of a spot to defend. Here Companies D and F relieved the survivors of Company A and C. They were joined by the Royal Scots, who alternated duty with them at the front, for the next two months, in defending against the Bolo advances.

My dearest ideal wife,

Your dear, sweet letters all came yesterday, and I feel so good, dear, to think that you are feeling in such good spirits. Bless you, dear heart: I love you so much that I can't begin to express it in words: and, dear, your joy when I get home will not be anywhere equal to mine, as you have the kiddies to love, and I have no one, so have saved up a supply that will simply smother you!

That's the way, dear. Take the bargains and the good times and make time pass the very best you can. You know, dear, that I want you to always hope for the best and always try to say and promise you the very best I can. I continue to dream of home. I wish, my dear, with all my heart, that I could say I was coming home right away, but the army's a funny proposition, and it's not easy to get back to Canada. I came very close. Had my arm been completely useless after France, I might well have been home. But as it was, only half no good meant I still had more work to do.

Things are rather tangled up now, but don't be discouraged in the least, as I am sure the break Is not far off. All through, dear, I've been what the boys call lucky but which I call blessed: and I'm sure that the Lord will continue to oversee everything as it should be and for the best. So, I am not worrying and don't get too impatient, though at times I'll confess, I get so lonely for you all that I almost go mad.

I'm completely fed up, by the way, with this King and Country stuff, and it is never again for me. All that is keeping the thing going now is the guys higher up who are making a fortune out of it and who are having the best time of their lives. Every man in the army is of the same opinion, and it's only because we must that we stick it out. A guy with a leg or arm cut off who is going to Canada is called a lucky cuss. No one cares a snap about whether the show keeps up or not. But after all, it's right that we do our duty to end this thing. I've done my best to follow my patriotism and conscience, and if it has been buried and obscured, I guess the army is to blame, so I won't worry.

Keep smiling dear and don't get impatient as all is coming our way. Our love for each other is the one and only thing. Kiss all the kiddies, dear.

Yours always,

Am

Before turning in for the night in Kitsa, after finishing another letter home to Florence, I opened my Book of Mormon, returning to Mosiah Chapter 7, another version of what I had read in Alma, to continue following the adventures of my namesake, Ammon, in the times before Christ.

The king Mosiah, having had a time of peace of 3 years, was preparing to send 16 men to Lehi-Nephi to check on their brethren who had gone off to the land of Zarahemla. Ammon, being strong and mighty, was chosen as leader. They travelled 40 days in the wilderness and pitched their tents on a hill north of Shilom.

Ammon and three of his brothers, travelled down to Nephi where they were captured and put in prison by the king's guard.

King Limhi, explained he was the son of Zeniff who originally came from Zarahemla, and had inherited this land and was made king by the voice of the people.

Aha, I thought! Perhaps this was an early democracy!

As in the book of Alma, Ammon explained who he was, this time explaining he was a descendent of Zarahemla, come out to inquire about his brethren.

The king was happy to learn who Ammon and his brethren were and outlined his people's plight at the hand of the Lamanites, who were taxing them grievously. Learning the Nephites could be an ally in freeing them from the Lamanites, he said he would rather be a slave to the Nephites than pay tribute to the Lamanites.

Freeing Ammon and his brethren, he planned an event the next day, bringing the people together at the temple. The next day he spoke to the gathering, telling them that the time was near when they would end the subjection by their enemies. He called for them to trust in God, who he described as the God of Abraham, Isaac and Jacob, and who had brought the children of Israel out of Egypt, allowed them to walk across the Red Sea and fed them with manna to keep them from starving in the wilderness.

Due to his people's iniquities and abominations, he explained, *they had been brought into bondage. When Zeniff, a previous king of his people, was trying to inherit the land of his fathers, he was tricked by king Laman, who created a treaty with Zeniff, giving up part of the land, including Lehi-Nephi and the city of Shilom and the surrounding area.*

At this point I thought about the treaty of Brest-Litovsk, in which the Bolsheviks had sacrificed large pieces of Russia to the Germans, just to achieve peace and gain breathing room to allow their revolution to survive.

So Limhi went on about the bondage by and tributes paid to the Lamanites and all the sorrows his people were suffering. Again, blaming their tribulations on their transgressions, he added that they even had fallen to fighting among themselves.

Here, in a foreshadowing of, perhaps, John the Baptist, and the coming Christ, he said "A prophet of the Lord have they slain; yea, a chosen man of God, who told them of their wickedness and abominations, and prophesied of many things which are to come, yea, even the coming of Christ." No wonder the people were in bondage, "smitten with sore afflictions"!

Finally, Limhi prepared to introduce Ammon to speak, saying "But if ye will turn to the Lord with full purpose of heart and put your trust in him with all diligence of mind, if ye do this, he will, according to his own will and pleasure, deliver you out of bondage."

During the epic escape from Shenkursk to Kitsa, I almost felt like Michael and Moroni were flying above us like a couple of heavenly biplanes, protecting us from the Bolshevik hordes behind us. Like opening the Red Sea for Moses, escaping the Pharoah's forces, they had created a path through the frozen wilderness. So finally in a truly deep sleep in Kitsa, I should have expected my angelic companions to appear.

They were framed, as usual, by snow covered evergreens, and blew 2 golden trumpets in unison. Their music heralded our success in escaping from our enemies. They spoke in loud voices, in unison.

"Praise God, Ammon, as you and your forces have been brought to safety on the road to the city of the Archangel. Your courage, your love of God, and the righteousness of your cause, have brought you salvation!"

Feeling somewhat sheepish, as usual, in their presence, I thanked them humbly for guiding us through the frozen wilderness.

"The refugees from Shenkursk, the wounded from our hospital, and all of our forces thank you for delivering us from certain destruction back in the city. I could feel your presence guiding us as we travelled through the forest!"

"Indeed, young Ammon. For we were and are with you, every inch of the journey," spoke Michael.

"As we are always," Moroni added. "You should know we, the angelic hosts, are with you always. We hear your thoughts and bring guidance like a telegram from the Lord."

I suddenly realized that not just in these momentary dreams and visions, but in every moment in my journey on earth, the angels were within me, guiding me and connecting me with God. With this reassurance and inspiration, I returned to dreamless sleep.

Chapter 8

Rest and Relaxation Back in Archangel

After surviving the November battles in Tulgas and the siege and evacuation of Shenkursk, I and some of the boys from the Canadian Artillery finally were rotated over for some time to rest and unwind in Archangel. As we had barely seen the city when we first arrived, we set out to get to know it better during our short stay there.

We were aware from our earlier visit that there were two ports for large ships in Archangel. One was Bakaritza, across the Dvina southwest from Archangel, from which we departed on the barges to Tulgas. The other, on the southeast side of the Dvina, was an area of docks in the suburb of Smolny, south of downtown Archangel. This area consisted of a huge wharf with large warehouses and housed the barracks of many of the Yanks. It, like much of Archangel, had cobblestone streets covered, now, with many inches of mud and snow.

The American camp was east of the main street of Archangel, Troitsy Prospect. This boulevard, like much of the city, was lit with electricity, with street cars running the length of it, north and south. Most of the streetcars were run by Russian women, except during the strike brought on by the overthrow of Chaikovsky's government by General Poole and Chaplin. At that point Yanks like Abe Vronsky, who was experienced as an operator from back home in Detroit, kept them running.

Coincidentally, and much to our pleasure, Abe was also in Archangel on leave the week we were there. He described life in the Yank barracks in Smolny as not that great. The muddy camp had filthy latrines and the drinking water wasn't fit to drink.

Of course, when we arrived in Archangel in early December, the snow had started taking over the mud in the camps, the Dvina had frozen over, and reindeer or pony driven sleighs could get us around town and across the river to Bakaritsa.

Some Yanks, permanently assigned to guard duty in Archangel, built a large structure several stories high, paving it with snow, creating a tall sloping run that would send small sleds flying out over the snow and onto the ice-covered Dvina. This provided quite an exciting ride indeed!

As in Shenkursk, the population of Archangel was much more varied than the primitive villages covering most of the province. When we first arrived, rich Russians, diplomats and former Tsarist officers walked the streets in all their finery. Some of the Archangel residents were quite wealthy, like those who owned the lumber mills and other industries. The American Headquarters was housed in the mansion of a former Russian sugar millionaire.

Though the Allies were supplying much of the food for the city, the Great War and the civil war meant many were struggling to make a living in the area. The people on the streets would range from those in fine suits and dresses to clothing stitched together out of burlap or flour sacking. Men's hats varied from derbies and top hats to tall woolen or fur hats like those of the Cossacks.

Due to General Poole's strategy in the intervention of recruiting Russians and training them to fight the Bolsheviks, many more British officers were in Archangel than it would take to command the modest British forces. Some were busy training the British Slavic Legion and other units, but many spent much of their time, along with ex-Tsarist officers and wealthy White Russian emigres from Moscow and St Petersburg, enjoying the bars, cafes and other pleasures of Archangel.

Among the pleasures or curses, of course, of any war zone in history, is prostitution. As many of the Russian women were desperate for cash or means to stay alive, they were forced into making themselves available for sex for the thousands of soldiers passing through Archangel. Establishments popular with the troops, including the Café de Paris, which Abe and I had already visited, featured waitresses, many of whom were also available for intimate services. Some establishments were made "off-limits" for the soldiers, but, as in any war, lonely men often turn to women, as well as drink, to find solace and relief from the stress of the battlefields.

I later heard that, per the Yanks' chief surgeon, the rate of venereal disease reported and treated in North Russia was about the same as or less than that of the American Expeditionary Force in France. That may be, partially, because so many of the Americans spent most of their time on the battle fronts and little time back in Archangel.

Abe and I, though, with wives and families back home, were not interested in these pleasures of the flesh, and spent no time with these women of the night. We did, however, find ways to entertain ourselves. The YMCA, of course, provided access to games, books, movies and tobacco. Other events were organized in Archangel including the already mentioned sled rides, boxing matches and musical and dramatic presentations in local halls.

The highpoint of Abe and my time in Archangel, however, was the amazing coincidence which led to a platonic date for dinner at the Café de Paris. In a twist of fate, after retreating with the wounded from Vistafka, Nurse Valentine had accompanied them to the American's hospital in Archangel. There she continued to work as one of the chief nurses. She also spent part of her time, however, as an interpreter for General Ironside and the British brass at headquarters.

When Abe and I went to the hospital to visit a buddy who was wounded back in Vistafka, not only was Nurse Valentine at the hospital, but so was the tall, dark beauty, Olga Menchofski, who saved the lives of the Allied wounded before losing her lover in the Battle of Tulgas. After having proved herself as a nurse for the Allies in Bereznik and Archangel, she and Nurse Valentine had met and become close friends. Hoping they could help us get to know Archangel, we invited them to dinner at the Café de Paris, the only restaurant we knew in Russia.

That evening I met Nurse Valentine (or Selma, as she preferred to be called) at British Naval Headquarters, where she was doing interpreting. She and I walked to the Café Paris where Abe and Olga would meet us for dinner at 7 after taking the streetcar from the hospital. As we walked, she told me the story of her first 36 years. She was born in 1893 in Russia. Her father was French-Ulster and her mother was Swedish-Russian. Her father, George Valentine, was grandson of a French nobleman who escaped from France during the revolution there and ended up on the Irish coast in a shipwreck. He married an Irish lass named Browne. When he came to the UK, they were tracking all the immigrants from revolutionary France, under the 1793 Aliens Act. The British feared that the social upheaval in France might spread to England. His name was listed in the alien registry created under the act.

George Valentine married the daughter of the governor of the Russian Baltic states of Lithuania and Estonia. George had been living in Belfast and had been educated at Rugby and Oxford. His wife, Selma's mother, had been educated at the Imperial School (known as the Smolny Institute) in St Petersburg. This was the first school in Russia for women of the aristocracy and taught etiquette, dancing, sewing, cooking, history and languages.

During the revolution in 1917 the Smolny Institute was made the Bolshevik party headquarters by Lenin. Selma, who had studied at Wordsworth in London and could speak Russian, English, French and German, returned to St Petersburg in 1916 and lived there through the Bolos' rise, hearing the speeches of Trotsky, Lenin and others.

After nursing in Shenkursk before the British arrived, she had served as an interpreter for the Royal Navy in Archangel and was made a petty officer. Then she returned to Shenkursk to tend the wounded before I met her on Thanksgiving and again on the night we made our dramatic escape from the Bolo siege of that city.

When we arrived at the Café De Paris, Abe and Olga had gotten a table and we joined them. In another coincidence, when they arrived they spotted Dugald McDougal, our RAF flyer friend, and asked him to join us. As Abe, Olga and Selma all spoke Russian, we jumped back and forth a bit between languages, but we first got a brief story about Olga's life, as we ordered drinks and dinner. We noticed though, in looking around, that the variety of food, due to shortages, had dramatically decreased in Archangel since the last time we had eaten at the Café de Paris.

Olga's story was as dramatic as Selma's, if not as international. Olga, who had taken her lover Menschovski's name after he died at the battle of Tulgas, was Russian, through and through. She grew up in the city of Tomsk in Siberia, daughter of a peasant family. She moved to St Petersburg before the Great War and worked in industrial plants. She joined the women's union that took to the streets igniting the revolution which overthrew the Tsar. Not particularly political, she enjoyed the drama and excitement of confronting the Tsar's cavalry in the streets during those tumultuous days.

As Kerensky's government struggled to stabilize the country in 1917, she met Maria Bochkareva, who also grew up in Tomsk, who was organizing a women's combat battalion to shame men of the Russian Army into getting back on the front lines in the fight against Germany. Given the go-ahead by Kerensky, then Minister of War, Maria began recruiting for the 1st Russian Women's Battalion of Death.

Learning about this unique unit, Olga joined 2,000 recruits in training for combat in St Petersburg. As the Bolsheviks and others were calling for peace following the Tsar's abdication, the Russian Army was beginning to fall apart. The Women's Battalion, however, joined the Kerensky Offensive, in the last battle against the Germans on Russia's western front in Smarhom. Maria and Olga were both wounded in the battle and returned to St Petersburg.

Then Olga and Maria's paths diverged. As the Bolsheviks took over in the fall revolution, Maria met and fell in love with a Bolshevik, Nickolyevich Melochofski. After the victory of the Reds in the revolution, Melochofski joined the growing Soviet army under Trotsky. This took Nick and Olga through Vologda to the Archangel province and the bloody battle in Tulgas.

In the meantime, now supporting the White Russian cause, and after being detained by the Bolsheviks in St Petersburg, Maria travelled to Omsk, to meet with General Kornilov, commander of the forces fighting their way towards Viatka to join the Allied forces in preparation of an assault on Moscow. Detained again by the Bolsheviks, she faced execution as a spy for the Whites. She managed to escape, however, and travelled to the U.S. to argue for American support of the White Russian cause.

She had gained fame as the commander of the Women's Battalion of Death, and was able to meet with President Wilson, who, hearing her case, had approved U.S. participation in the intervention in North Russia.

Ironically, Olga noted, now that she was serving the Allies in the hospital in Archangel, her old friend and commander, Maria, had arrived to meet with Ironside and allied leadership. She was offering, again, to organize women for the White Russian combat units being organized to fight the Bolsheviks. British leadership, however, didn't take her seriously, and she wandered the city in her Russian uniform, a sad and disheveled soldier who was readier than most of the Russian men, to fight the Bolsheviks.

When General Ironside met with her, he noted "She presented a pathetic figure, with greying untidy hair, and looking much older than she really was. Her broad ugly face, mottled complexion and squat figure showed clearly her Eastern heritage. Tears came to her eyes when she told me that she served her country well, but the Provisional government would have nothing to do with her. She wished to serve against the Bolsheviks, who were ruining her country."

Ironside sent her over to White Russian General Marousheffsky. She met with him to plead her case. His Order of the Day regarding her request to join the fight against the Bolos was discouraging. In it he noted "I consider that the summoning of women for military duties, which are not appropriate for their sex, would be a heavy reproach and a disgraceful stain on the whole population of the northern region. I order that Madame Botchkareva take off her uniform."

Having heard the dramatic stories of our two female companions, and with our lives being so much less interesting, Abe, Dugald and I continued to eat, drink and be merry and told the stories of our brief lives.

Abe's family, like many turn-of-the-century Jewish Eastern Europeans, had moved to America due to the wars, social upheaval and pogroms of the old world. Arriving first in New York, his family soon moved to the growing industrial center of Detroit. As many Eastern Europeans, his father had mechanical skills and eventually found work in the growing automobile industry, working for Henry Ford. When Abe finished school, he worked briefly for Ford, but then found work on the streetcar lines of the city.

As the streetcars joined railroads as unionized work, Abe became a member of the union, and was active in it's politics. Not as radical as an IWW "Wobbly", Abe still believed, with many in the labor movement, that the owners and "capitalists" in America and around the world received and owned much more than their fair share of the wealth produced by the workers. As a proud union member, too, he had mixed feelings about serving as a "scab" in replacing the women streetcar drivers in Archangel, when they had gone on strike.

Much more concerning to him, though, was the fact that, as

Allied soldiers, we had been sent to Russia to fight our fellow workers. We were here to defeat the Bolsheviks, a group trying to design a society that treated the workers and the peasants more fairly than they had been treated for centuries under the Tsars.

The new government was not what you would call a democracy and, under the Red Terror, was killing and torturing many of its citizens and enemies. But to come under the pretense of rebuilding the Eastern Front and guarding the allies' military supplies, and then to be sent out to shoot other workers and peasants in the northern forests, didn't sit well with Abe.

Later, of course, we would learn other allied troops were questioning this intervention, and sometimes even resorted to protests, work stoppages and mutinies, to express their beliefs.

After blowing off steam about his feelings about workers' rights and our role in Russia,
Abe finished his biography by sharing photos of his wife and two kids back in Detroit.

Finally, our flyer friend, Captain MacDougal, gave a brief view of his young life. Being 23 years old and single, he was the only worthy bachelor in the group, and Abe and I were a little worried he might catch the eye of our two young lady guests. He told us he was born and raised in Lockport, Manitoba, an unincorporated village on the Red River 17 miles north of Winnepeg. In recent years a big dam and bridge was built there which got rid of some rapids and made the river more navigable for boats wanting to reach Lake Winnipeg. The dam was the only "curtain style" bridge in North America. It meant that, mobile "curtains" could be rolled back before the freeze in the winter, preventing ice jams, and permitting flood waters to flow through during the spring. For those of us dealing with the freezing Russian rivers all winter, we could appreciate this.

Dugald had been a Railroad clerk before, like me, volunteering for the Canadian infantry and going to France. After we had met in the trenches at Vimy Ridge, he, like me, decided to get out of the infantry and all of the dangers of going "over the top." He entered an RAF training facility and learned to fly. He did some flying in France, and, when given the opportunity to volunteer for the North Russian force, jumped at it.

He talked about how much he liked flying the seaplanes launched off of the HMS Nairana. The Nairana, originally built as a ferry to be used in Tasmania, was converted to an aircraft carrier with a runway for biplanes on the bow, and cranes to lift seaplanes into the water on the stern. The use of this kind of ship, and the use of a combination of seaplanes, naval artillery and ground troops, was what made the successful attack on the Mudyug artillery battery a first in history.

After his dramatic flyover of Archangel, sending the Bolos packing, he became one of the most famous flyers in the RAF flights serving in North Russia. He won several decorations, and spent time based in Beresnik, supporting allied efforts on the Dvina. He hoped to continue flying after the war and appreciated the opportunity to be a part of making history.

By the time we had heard Selma, Olga, Abe and Dugald's stories, we were enjoying dessert and brandy and I briefly shared my life story, as both Abe and Selma, had heard much of it before. I summarized how I was a Mormon, how that differed from other Christian sects, how it had historical roots in the Book of Mormon, delivered by an angel to Joseph Smith, written on golden plates, and summarizing the lost tribes of Israel and their travels and battles in the New World. I talked about the angel Moroni, and the historical character named Ammon, who had been part of all of this. I explained I had grown up among Mormons in McGrath, Alberta, Canada to become a teamster and then a schoolteacher.

I then showed pictures of my loving wife, Florence, and our 3 children, Luana, Maxine and Kay Lloyd. They had all recently survived the Spanish flu, for which I would be eternally grateful. I joked that Florence had learned to heal almost every ailment with "consecrated" olive oil and was sure she would have used it for the flu.

Florence, or Fife, as I called her, for the Scottish town from which her ancestors had come, had received a "Patriarchal Blessing" from Patriarch E.H. Blackburn in Loa, Utah, before moving to Canada. He had taught her about this consecrated oil and said she would have "dreams, visions and revelations" of things to come. She did, indeed, from then on, in her life. When I was wounded at Vimy Ridge, for example, she saw it all in a dream, including seeing blood on my shoulder. The next day she received a wire letting her know I was wounded but had survived.

As we finished our dessert, we agreed we had certainly gotten to know each other better. We wished each other well as we knew Selma, Abe, Dugald and I, as British, American and Canadian citizens, would soon be setting sail for our homes. Abe, Dugald and I would be going back to our families and jobs in North America. Selma, she shared, had volunteered to, after the evacuation and visiting her family home in Ireland, travel with the Brits to areas being fought for by the White Russians in Southern Russia. General Poole, who had been in charge in Archangel at the beginning of the intervention, was active in supporting the Volunteer Army and Cossacks fighting the Reds down there.

Dugald interrupted, however, and said he had decided, as well, that, as he was serving in the RAF, to volunteer to keep flying with the relief forces attacking the Bolsheviks, while the rest of the Allies would be sailing for home.

Olga, she said, would also stay with General Miller's forces, and continue to serve as a nurse and do what she could to alleviate the suffering of her countrymen, as the Civil War played out. Little did she know that in the spring of 1920, after we Allies had left, General Miller's forces would be quickly overwhelmed, and many of the White Russians in Archangel would be executed. Years later we learned that this brave and impetuous woman managed to survive and find her way back to Tomsk, where she lived out her life to a ripe old age as a nurse and a citizen of the Union of Soviet Socialist Republics.

Bidding each other farewell, Olga and Selma made their way back to their quarters, and Abe, Dugald and I headed back to our respective barracks, having been complete gentlemen with our female companions, in one of the most popular centers of prostitution in Archangel.

My dearest wife:

I dreamed I was home last night and wish to God it was true. I feel like I would love you enough to satisfy your dear loving heart. As we are now safe in Archangel I was able to sleep so well I had the best rest I have had in months and felt Jake in the morning.

You will be glad to know we are away from the war zone, and soon will be shipping off to Merry Old England and back home to Canada.

Abe, Dugald and I had dinner with two girls we know from our time in Russia. I mentioned before, Nurse Valentine, who helped tend the wounded in the evacuation of Shenkursk, and Olga Menchovski, who saved the wounded soldiers' lives in the hospital in Tulgas. This will be last time we will see them as we will ship out soon.

As I said before, you should never worry in the least, as there is only one girl in the world that has the love of my heart. Well, two more little ones, Luana and Maxine, who go with her, of course!

Bless you my dearest. If you could read my heart, you wouldn't worry one bit about my love being true. I do wonder, sometimes, how your love survived the time when I was such a fool. That is all in the past now, and I will be a husband and father to be proud of when I return to your arms. Have faith—I am coming home soon

As ever, dear,

Am

When I turned in at the Archangel barracks, my mind buzzed with the conversations with my friends at dinner. What a strange world and what a strange war had brought us together in this God forsaken place. Writing my usual apologies to Fife for having spent time with attractive young ladies, I finally settled down to read. I pulled out my dog-eared Book of Mormon, opening it to the Mosiah, Chapter 8

After king Limhi had spoken to his people, he had Ammon stand before the multitude to speak of the history of his brethren. When he finished the king dismissed the multitude and he had the plates with the record of his people from the time they left the land of Zarahemla and asked Ammon to read them.

Ammon read the records, but the king wanted to know if he could interpret languages, which Ammon said he could not.

The king explained how he had sent his people to find Zarahemla, and how, in a land of bones of men and beasts and ruins of buildings, they discovered the remnants of a people who were as numerous as the tribes of Israel. From this land, they had brought back 24 plates, engraved with messages, of pure gold, as well as ancient breast plates of brass and copper.

Limhi asked Ammon if he knew anyone who could translate the plates.

Ammon replied that he did, indeed, know such a man. This ability to translate, he said, was a gift from God. It was accomplished with a device call an "interpreter", which only certain individuals could use. If using this device for the wrong purpose, one would perish. But those who were able to use the interpreter were deemed as "seers." The king of the land of Zarahemla, he said, is that man who had this "high gift" from God.

Limhi said the seer must be greater than a prophet.

Ammon replied that a seer is a "revelator" and a prophet also. This, he said, is the greatest gift a man can have, unless he has the power of God, which no man does. But great powers can be given a man by God.

Further, he noted, that a seer may know things of the past, the future and know secrets which are made manifest, bringing hidden things to light. A seer then makes unknown things known.

God had given this power to seers in order that they, through faith, could work miracles and provide benefits to their fellow men.

The king was thrilled to hear these marvelous works of God and lamented that mankind often doesn't seek this wisdom. "Yea, they are as a wild flock which fleeth from the shepherd, and scattereth, and are driven and devoured by the beasts of the forest."

Before we finished our leave in Archangel, the first of many mutinies by the newly trained White Russian troops occurred. The 1st Archangel Regiment's commander, General Marousheffsky, was ordered by Ironside to mobilize his troops to take their place on the front. At dinner the night before calling the mobilization, the General warned there would be trouble, but Ironside insisted the men must be called out the next day.

Ordered to parade for Ironside at 11 am outside of the Alexander Nevsky Barracks, 2,000 infantrymen refused to come out, and began waving red flags from the windows. Ironside immediately surrounded the barracks with British troops, announcing that the nearby Archangel residents should go to their homes. Meanwhile, Marousheffsky, who Ironside viewed as incompetent, was running about shouting orders to burn the barracks down.

Taking him aside, Ironside explained he would prefer to save the lives of the bulk of the soldiers, but just deal with the ringleaders of the mutiny. As the Russian general continued to shout incoherently, Ironside sent him away and strode up to the perimeter of troops surrounding the barracks. The Colonel in charge said that all the White Russian troops were in the barracks and that they hadn't harmed their officers.

To let the rebellious troops know he was serious, Ironside called for some Lewis gun fire in multiple bursts to break a few of the barracks' windows. An exchange of shots was fired towards and from the building, and more red flags were waved out of the windows. Ironside wondered how they had found so much red cloth on short notice!

Then Ironside had a class of Russian officers who had been practicing with Stokes mortars set up around the building and lob two rounds. One round fell in an inner quadrangle and one on the roof. Before another shot could be fired the doors flew open and hundreds of men ran out with hands raised, surrendering en masse. Meanwhile, the red flags fell from the windows and the mutiny had ended.

Ironside was chuckling at the stupidity of the attempted rebellion. The troops fell in and were formed into companies on the parade ground. In Russian Ironside bellowed "I want the ringleaders of this mutiny to fall out immediately!" Thirteen stepped forward without hesitation. When he queried as to whether there were any more ringleaders, the thirteen yelled "Nyet!!" in unison. The rest of the gathered troops affirmed this, also yelling "Nyet!" Ironside looked at the troops quizzically as if he found the whole affair quite strange.

In his diary, Ironside noted that the 13 men were shot that afternoon after a trial by their Russian officers. In later years, however, in his memoires, he noted that the sentences were actually commuted, and that the men later gained their freedom. Either way, in his commanding style, Ironside effectively quelled a Bolshevik inspired mutiny. Unfortunately, as the North Russian intervention continued, other mutinies broke out which the Allies couldn't control.

The need for newly trained White Russian troops, however, was critical. Despite assuming they would be digging in for the winter, the Bolsheviks began offensives, including on the Dvina. There the Sixth Red Army under the command of N.N. Kuzmin was attacking. Though the Royal Scots, the Americans and the Canadian artillery had held them off in November in Tulgas, more troops were arriving and threatening the allied positions.

Fortunately, to meet the growing Bolo threat, in December and January, 4500 new White Russian trainees grew to nearly 6,000, almost half of whom were being rotated to assist the units on several of the 5 fingered fronts. With more recruiting, the Russian forces grew to 12,000 fighters.

While the Brits trained more White Russians, many of whom mutinied, even the U.S. troops began to protest and mutiny. Sergeant Parrish Silver, still stationed in Tulgas months after the Armistice Day battle, had begun to get fed up with how things were going in North Russia. He still felt lousy about having directed his troops to burn the village of Upper Tulgas, but now had even more bones to pick with the way the war was being run.

In early March he and his troops circulated a petition with grievances against their leadership and threatening to refuse to do sentry and patrol duty. They listed a number of issues. One was that they were not getting enough artillery support. Another was that, with the Dvina ice melting soon, they would be sitting ducks when the Bolo gunboats returned downriver. Other issues in the petition, signed by 50 Yank soldiers, were asking "why we are fighting Bolos, why we haven't any big guns, why the English run us, why we haven't enough to eat and why men can't get proper medical attention."

In response to the petition, Sergeant Parrish was read the Articles of War by British Colonel Graham, informing him that organizing this mutinous petition was punishable by death. As he was up for an English Military Medal from General Ironside himself, however, for his bravery, Parrish ended up facing no punishment. He did, however, have more comments on the way the war was being run, in his diary notes:

"The majority of the people here are in sympathy with the Bolos and I don't blame them. In fact, I am 9/10 Bolo myself, and they all call me the Bolo: and my platoon the Bolo platoon, because every man in the platoon signed that petition against fighting the Bolos after the Germans had quit."

He pointed out, however, that "We have got the best fighting record of any platoon in the Battalion. So we shouldn't worry and get home."

The Bolsheviks, of course, were wont to encourage the feelings of soldiers like Sgt Parrish, who felt some sympathy for working class revolutionaries who had wrested governing power from the rich and the industrialists in Russia. Back home, as union members especially, they had their share of fights with the "ruling class."

A Bolshevik propaganda organ called The Call, published in Moscow, was distributed to the troops in North Russia. Many might ignore it, but some of our boys might have seen some logic in cases made in arguments like these:

"You soldiers are fighting on the side of the employers against us, the working people of Russia. All this talk about intervention to 'save' Russia amounts to this, that the capitalists of your countries, are trying to take back from us what we won from their fellow capitalists in Russia. Can't you realize that this is the same war that you have been carrying on in England and America against the master class? You hold the rifles, you work the guns to shoot us with, and you are playing the contemptible part of the scab. Comrade, don't do it!"

"You are kidding yourself that you are fighting for your country. The capitalist class places arms in your hands. Let the workers cease using these weapons against each other, and turn them on their sweaters. The capitalists themselves have given you the means to overthrow them, if you had but the sense and the courage to use them. There is only one thing that you can do: arrest your officers. Send a commission of your common soldiers to meet our own workingmen, and find out yourselves what we stand for."

"Do you British working-men know what your capitalists expect you to do about the war? They expect you to go home and pay in taxes figured into the price of your food and clothing, eight thousand millions of English pounds or forty thousand millions of American dollars. If you have any manhood, don't you think it would be fair to call all these debts off? If you think this is fair, then join the Russian Bolsheviks in repudiating all war debts.

Or:

"Do you realize that the principle reason the British-American financiers have sent you to fight us for, is because we were sensible enough to repudiate the war debts of the bloody, corrupt old Czar?

Before we finished our leave in Archangel, Abe and I volunteered for one brief mission that proved educational. A group of soldiers from the 339th was asked to take a newly arrived group of Bolshevik prisoners to the prison built and operated by the French on Mudyug Island. Having nothing else to do, I came along, as we boarded a British vessel in Bakaritza transporting us to the island prison.

Mudyug, an island in the Dvina River delta facing the White Sea, was a long-time lighthouse site, and had been the location of the air-sea-land battle Dugald fought in as the allies first arrived in Archangel. As we unloaded 100 prisoners captured in action by the Australians on the Railroad Front, we noted the huge Naval guns mounted on the beach, which had dueled with the Allies when they arrived.

The prisoner of war camp, large wooden sheds surrounded by barbed wire fences, held Bolshevik prisoners going back to when the British first arrived and rounded up any Bolos still in the city. With the tide too low to reach the docks, the prisoners were unloaded on the beach in waist deep water and were escorted as they walked ashore by rifle carrying French guards. Proceeding up the beach we were attacked by typical swarms of North Russian mosquitos.

Walking the prisoners into their quarters, we noticed the multiple decked wooden bunks, with no mattresses or cushions, which they would now call home. Many of the prisoners were young, in their mid to late teens. Some looked like typical Russian peasants, but others looked like idealistic young college students or socialists who had gotten caught up in the drama of the Bolshevik revolution.

One blond young chap looked particularly angelic and idealistic. How, one felt like asking, did such a nice young man become part of a movement trying to overthrow all of the world's capitalist governments?

111

Abe chatted with him briefly in Russian, and he explained he had been a student in St Petersburg, participated in the revolution, and was assigned to help in setting up the Bolshevik bureaucracy in Archangel. When the British arrived, he, and hundreds of others, were locked up in train cars in Bakaritsa, then transported to Mudyug Island.

Years later, when I read about the Gulags in the Soviet Union, I found it somewhat ironic that one of the first prison camps in post-revolutionary Russia was built and maintained by the French and other allied troops.

But cest la vie and cest la guerre, I suppose.

Chapter 9

Bolshie Ozerki-Cutting Off the 5th Finger

Of the 5 fingers of the Allies' North Russian intervention, the quietest through most of the winter, was Onega. The front defended the key communication and supply line between Murmansk and Obozerskaya and the railway north to Archangel. The brilliant Bolshevik General Kuropatkin, who had dueled with Ironside throughout the winter of 1918 with parries and thrusts against multiple lines of defense, now struck on the Onega Front. He sent a flanking force east of the railroad above Obozerskaya. On March 16 his forces attacked an unprepared French base at the village of Bolshie Ozerki, on the road between the Railroad Front and Onega, wiping them out and capturing a supply convoy.

A village priest escaped to Obozerskaya, letting allied headquarters know the Bolsheviks had flanked the whole Railroad Front and would soon be attacking. General Ironsides, seeing this was to be a key battle, travelled down from Archangel immediately to take command. Learning that a French force in Chanova, west of Bolshie Ozerki, had been cut off in an attempt to attack the Bolos, Ironside ordered a company of Yorks and other forces to travel down from Onega to join Yanks there and prepare an attack.

On March 18, Lt Collins of H Company (30 Yanks and a Lewis gun) was escorting French Colonel Lucas to within 4 versts west of Bolshie Ozerki in sleighs when they were attacked by Bolo machine guns from the village. Lucas' sleigh was overturned, throwing him in the snow but the Yanks returned fire, losing one man in the exchange. Retreating by crawling through the snow, they returned to Chanova, with several cases of frostbite, digging in in case the Bolos followed.

Under Ironside's orders, the 300 Yorks (who were in route from Murmansk to reinforce the Railroad Front at Obozerskaya) and 40 H Company Yanks from Onega, arrived to reinforce an attack on Bolshie Ozerki. Little did they know they were outnumbered by 5 to 1 by the Bolsheviks they faced.

The troops moved out at 2 am. The Yanks took the middle and one company each of the Yorks moved up on the left and right flanks. Another York company was held in reserve. By 0900, the Yanks took heavy machine gun fire. Trudging 500 yards in deep snow, they bogged down but held a line 100 yards from the Bolos. The Yorks also advanced, taking fire. After 5 hours, Lt Collins was mortally wounded while cheering his troops on. Lt Phillips reported that his company was almost out of ammunition and needed reinforcements. Colonel Lawrie ordered a retreat, and all fell back by nightfall. One Yank and Lt Collins died in the action, and 8 Yanks were badly wounded. The Yorks suffered 4 killed and 10 wounded. Both units suffered multiple cases of frostbite.

Now realizing that the enemy far outnumbered them, and was fortifying their position with barbed wire, more machine guns, artillery and additional troops, the British-American force in Chanova called for reinforcements from Onega before attacking again.

In the meantime, General Kuropatkin's force at Bolshie Ozerki began attacking the Americans and White Russian forces between them and Obozerskaya. He surrounded them with 3 regiments, and after 2 days of repeated attacks, was threatening to wipe them out.

Colonel Lawrie, with his mixed force in Bolshie Ozerki, was ordered to attack to take pressure off the units blocking the Bolsheviks drive towards Obozerskaya. Several Yank platoons, a company of Yorks and a Polish unit moved up for an attack at 3 am. Bolo dogs, kept in the forest, barked and announced the surprise attack. Machine gun fire killed one of the British officers and drove back all into the deep snow. By 6 am Yanks were sent forward to cover the retreat of the Yorks.

The Polish unit, which showed up late, was supposed to do a flank attack under cover of a Yank mortar barrage, but, taking losses from heavy machine gun fire, also retreated. The Polish force refused to go forward again, and a line of Brits and Yanks held off a Bolshevik counterattack till nightfall.

Though they made no ground, the Allied forces in Chanova continued to harass the Soviet forces in their bid to breakthrough to Obozerskaya. They lost 11 killed and 28 wounded among the Yanks, Brits and Poles in the action.

While the forces west of Bolshie Ozerki were harassing the Bolsheviks there, Ironside was building up his forces between the Reds and Obozerskaya. From Archangel, to start, he brought one American regiment, 80 Yorks and the French Legion Courier du Bois (White Russians trained by the French). When these initial troops attacked, the Bolo artillery sent the White Russians into a panic as E Company of the Yanks struggled in deep snow trying to approach the Reds. In this first advance, they could hear the firing from the engagement by H Company on the other side of the village.

For a few days the Allies and the Reds brought more artillery up to the Bolshie Ozerki battlefield. More White Russians and Americans reinforced the allied position 18 versts from the

Soviets. As the soldiers shivered in the deep snow, the 310 Engineers helped fortify the position with barricades of logs and two blockhouses, rapidly assembled. Working with Company M, the relatively green, French trained White Russians began to become more confident, as they practiced on machine guns and stocked the base with ammunition, food and artillery shells.

Meanwhile, the now 7,000 Soviet troops began their attack. General Kuropatkin's strategy was to overrun the allied defenses, move his artillery up the road and be able to bombard the allied base at Obozerskaya, his ultimate goal. For the initial attack on the Allies at Verst 18 he threw in 3 entire regiments- the 2nd Moscow, the 90th Saratov and the 2nd Kazan.

On March 31, with some troops approaching on skis, a Bolo surprise attack in the rear attempted to capture 2 French 75's guarded by Company M and the White Russian machine guns. Taking a page from the battle of Tulgas, the artillery officer reversed his guns and fired shrapnel into the charging Reds. An American corporal then took on two Bolo machine guns with his Lewis gun, silencing them.

With the diversion of this rear attack, the Soviets then attacked the forward blockhouses and barricades manned by the Yanks (fortunately) and not the green Russian trainees from Archangel trained by the French. The strength and accuracy of the American's fire caused great losses to the attacking Reds. Feeling confident, the Yanks replenished ammunition on the barricades. From captured Bolos, however, they learned this was an attack testing the Americans lines of fire, and the wave of Soviets, the next day, would be much stronger.

On April 1st, indeed, the Bolos attacked in three strong frontal waves, as well as action on the rear. This time the White Russian artillery began to rake the charging Reds with shrapnel with devastating accuracy. That, machine gun, Lewis gun, rifle fire and rifle grenades cut down wave after wave of attacking Bolos. By nightfall, all in the battle were suffering from extreme cold, but the Bolsheviks, lying in the snow where they had faltered and dug in, suffered the most. Some, fearing retreat more than surrender, crawled in and gave themselves up.

In a surreal moment out of a comedy Kinescope, the Bolsheviks' commanding officer, thinking that a midday pause in the fighting indicated a surrender of the Allied position, rode his white horse dramatically forward towards the Yanks' barricade with his sword raised, only to be picked off by a shot by one of the Doughboys.

The next day 2 heavy Bolo artillery barrages destroyed one of the barricades, sending the Allied troops, initially, back to cover behind the tree line. But the Soviet infantry attack barely lasted till noon that day. In the distance the Allies could hear H Company, the Yorks and the Poles, west of Bolshie Ozerki, in an unsuccessful attack against the Bolos. This took at least some of the enemy's attention. Meanwhile the Allies to their east continued to pound the Bolos with artillery for the rest of the day, littering the ground with dead.

By mid-April, realizing a warming in the weather was creating muddy roads which would make a retreat with artillery difficult, General Kuropatkin decided discretion would be the better part of valor for the five thousand surviving Red troops. They had been fought to a standstill in Bolshie Ozerki. Having lost over 2,000 men and wanting to move south while he could still save his artillery, he ordered a retreat. The entire force fled the region, leaving the key allied base at Obozerskaya safe for the moment. And, as the Bolos retreated, American General Wilds Richardson was on his way to Archangel to assist in the withdrawal of American troops from North Russia. The French forces began to be withdrawn into Archangel immediately in preparation for leaving, as well. The end of the intervention was approaching!

The retreat of the Bolos from Bolshie Ozerki also coincided with pulling out troops from various of the North Russia sectors. Many of these troops were sent to join Bolshevik forces fighting the Siberian anti-Bolshevik forces fighting their way towards Moscow led by General Kolchak and General Deniken's forces, aided by allied flyers, approaching Moscow from the southeast. These two major advances by the Whites were much more of a threat to the Reds than the allies defending their precarious positions in North Russia. This was especially true as the Americans and Canadians would be pulling out soon, as likely would all the allied forces before the fall freeze.

For Ironside, however, his plans continued to be to strengthen his five fronts for the final disengagement. Before returning to Archangel from the Railroad Front, he oversaw the transport of newly arrived 60 pounder artillery pieces to the critical Dvina front. Captain Stuart of the Canadian Artillery had overseen building oversized sleighs by the Navy and training of the Russian horses to pull them. The guns were so large that each one took a 10-horse sleigh, each trail and carriage had a 10-horse sleigh, each "buffer" had a 6-horse sleigh, each wheel was on a 10-horse sleigh and ammunition was carried in 50 1-horse sleighs. To move the 2 guns up to the Dvina front, it took 118 horses in all! These big guns would help in the Allies push to drive back the Bolos in preparation for a safe journey home.

One funny story shared by the Yanks in the 339th about the Bolshie Ozerkie front had to do with one of the British soldiers captured by the Bolsheviks. Actually, many of the Allies who were captured by the Red's were treated quite well. They were often sent down to Moscow and had the run of the city. They received a small stipend to live on and were encouraged to experience the Russian culture there and attend speaker events to learn how Bolshevism was succeeding.

In the funny story, however, the prisoner had a different fate. Father Roach, an Irish chaplain with the Brits, was proceeding to Bolshie-Ozerki to tend to the wounded. Not realizing the Bolos were there, he ended up getting captured. He was transferred down to Emtsa, the Bolo railroad base.

The regional commissar then proceeded to question him in French, as this was a language they shared. Trying to make friends with the commissar, with true Irish wit, he feigned interest in the Bolshevik doctrines. Within an hour he convinced the commissar that he was fully in support of Bolshevism. The commissar proposed that he would send the chaplain to Moscow where he could live comfortably and learn more about how he could help with the Bolshevik revolution.

Knowing going to Moscow might be as uncomfortable a journey as his trip from Bolshie-Ozerki to Emptsa, the chaplain suggested that he might do more good for the workers of the world by going back and preaching Bolshevism to the British troops.

The commissar agreed, and after treating Father Roach to a delicious meal of dried fish, beef, sour cream cheese and caviar, he transported the chaplain back to a blindfolded prisoner exchange with the Brits, with pockets full of Soviet propaganda.

The Irish chaplain, of course, conveniently failed in his mission as a propogandist, but shared the Bolshevik literature for the education and amusement of the British troops.

My darling wife:

I am getting so impatient now that our duty in North Russia has almost come to an end. We have been doing yeoman's work preparing our Russian friends to continue their work after we have gone.

I am much more restless than I have ever been before. I can't share the details, but we are getting close to finishing the work which brought us here.

In your letter you said you hope I get home by summer, or at least by the fall. It looks like we may be home by then for sure! I will be coming home in good healthy condition and want to find you, dear, and all the kiddies, in the same. I love you all, dear, and feel good all over that I'm so blessed. I dreamed about coming home last night, and that Roy's parents cut me cold. I guess I am imagining things, because after I wrote to them last year they wrote back with thanks for my condolences after he died in France.

Please, dear, don't worry about things. Keep well and happy and all will be well.

With love and kisses to all until I see you again.

Your loving

Am

In what was becoming a habit, perhaps for the good, I finished my darling wife's letter and returned to the Book of Alma, Chapter 27.

Finally, the Lamanites discovered, their struggles to destroy the Nephites in war was in vain and they returned to the land of Nephi. And the Amalekites, because of their loss, were angry and they began to destroy the Anti-Nephi-Lehi people.

Ammon and his brethren, seeing those who they loved, and those who had loved them, as if they were angels from God sent to protect them, felt compassion and said to their king that the people of the Lord should be gathered together to go down to Zarahemla, land of the Nephites, and flee out of the hands of their enemies.

Ammon offered to ask the Lord if this was the best plan, and, if he learned it was, asked if the king would go down "unto our brethren."

The king said they would go down if told to do so by the Lord and was prepared to serve as slaves to the people to pay back sins committed against them.

Ammon said that his father had created a law within the brethren that slavery was forbidden, so proposed to go down and rely on the mercies of the brethren.

The king again agreed to go if the Lord demanded it.

When Ammon asked the Lord, the Lord said that they should, indeed, get out of this land, for Satan was holding the hearts of the Amalekites, who had stirred up the Lamanites to anger against the brethren to kill them. The Lord blessed the people of this generation and promised to preserve them.

Ammon spoke with the king and they gathered all the people of the Lord and their flocks and herds, and left the land, traveling through the wilderness dividing the land of Nephi from the land of Zarahemla.

Leaving the people to wait at the border, Ammon and his brethren met Alma in a joyful meeting. So great was Ammon's joy that he was full and swallowed up in the joy of God, falling exhausted to the ground.

Alma, who also felt joy, brought his brethren into Zarahemla, to his own home. They met with the chief judge and related the things that had happened in the land of Nephi, among the Lamanites.

The chief judge then proclaimed throughout the land that their brethren, the people of Anti-Nephi-Lehi should be admitted into their land and given the land of Jershon, east by the sea, adjoining the land of Bountiful.

Their armies would be placed between the land of Jershon and the land Nephi, to protect their brethren in that land, as *they would fear taking up arms lest they commit a sin. This great fear came as they were feeling the need for repentance because of their wickedness and murders.*

Ammon returned to the people of Anti-Nephi-Lehi and explained they would be given the land of Jershon and they felt great joy and proceeded to take possession of the land there. The Nephites then began to call them the people of Ammon.

The people of Ammon were part of the church of God. They were distinguished by their zeal towards God and men. They were honest, upright and firm in their faith in Christ.

They looked on shedding the blood of their brethren with abhorrence and would not take up arms against them. They did not fear death, as the believed in Christ and the resurrection.

"And thus, they were a zealous and beloved people, a highly favored people of the Lord."

Chapter 10

Beating Back the Bolos For A Safe Journey Home

Despite Soviet troops' transfers to other fronts in the Russian civil war, plenty of Bolos remained on the 5 fronts in the province to make the Allies' lives miserable as they prepared their retreat to Archangel and embarkation through the White Sea. But, with the White Sea and the rivers thawing, help was on the way for the Allied forces.

Along with American General Wilds P. Richardson, who had served 20 years in Alaska, and who would be in charge of the Yank's embarkation, two British generals and their brigades, arrived with the British North Russia Relief Force. One was

George Grogan, a decorated veteran of service in battles in France including (being wounded at) Neuve Chapelle, the Somme and the Aisne. The other was General Sadleir-Jackson, a soldier Ironside knew from their days together in South Africa. Ironside viewed him as an ideal commander to lead the forces recruited to attack the Bolsheviks in disengagement efforts prior to the Brits leaving North Russia.

But before the first relief forces arrived, the thawing Dvina, helped by gigantic Allied dynamite charges near Archangel, had begun to create activity upriver on the Dvina front. Before British gunboats could get upriver, however, a White Russian unit, the 2nd Battalion of the North Russian Rifle Regiment, on the left bank of the Dvina near Tulgas, mutinied. Joined by the Bolshevik forces they had been facing, they turned on the loyal members of the battalion and a Russian Artillery unit. Retreating in the face of the Reds and the mutineers, the battalion survivors and the artillery, dragging two guns, retreated to a village downstream. With the help of my Canadian artillery unit stationed there, though, we drove the Bolos and the mutineers back upriver, in 48 hours of intense engagement.

This mutiny, not a good sign in terms of the ability of the White Russian troops to perform under fire, worried Ironside and British leadership. The dice had been rolled, however, in terms of bringing in relief forces to assist the Russians in fighting their own war with the Bolos, in preparation for the Allies move to leave North Russia.

Grogan's Brigade arrived in Archangel on May 26th. When their ships entered the Dvina, a tug carrying Ironside met them in the channel. Pulling up to the leading ship, Ironside gazed at the fresh faced young British soldiers, and one cried out "'ave you got any beer 'ere?" Ironsides chuckled as these young men, just in from England, had no idea they were entering a "beleaguered city at the end of a siege."

As Piskoff later explained it, when Ironside climbed on board

122

in his gunner's pea coat and black fishermen's boots, striding like a giant across the deck to meet the much shorter, rotund and cheerful General Grogan, one of the men called out "Lord love me, I shouldn't like him to hit me!"

As Ironside met Grogan, who was wearing his Victoria Cross, the general explained his men were well trained, fit and first-class soldiers who had been too young to serve in France. They had been formed into two battalions- the Hampshires and the Oxford and Bucks Light Infantry, both of which he was confident would do well. He had also brought a unit of mountain howitzers.

The next day Grogan's Brigade marched into Archangel to cheering crowds. 20,000 people came out to see the relief troops. Grogan met Generals Marousheffsky and Miller, the Russian commanders who would be taking up the fight when the allies left Russia. There was a traditional presentation of bread and salt on platters. Streamers with messages of welcome fluttered gayly.

Despite the crowd's enthusiasm, however, Ironside mused that, with all these loyal Russians in Archangel, it was frustrating that so few had signed up for the White Russian units the allies struggled to recruit and train to fight the Bolsheviks.

On the 30th of May Ironside received a personally dictated message from the King, which was read to more cheers at the head of the regiment:

"General Ironside,

I had many anxieties about your isolated forces at the commencement of the long Arctic Winter, but as time wore on these anxieties were allayed by the splendid way in which you have faced and mastered all difficulties.

On the arrival of the special relief contingent, I desire to congratulate you and your troops, together with their Allied and Russian comrades, on their achievements in the face of so many hardships, difficulties and perils. I wish also to assure you of the interest with which I shall continue to watch your operations, and may a good luck attend you.

George R.I.
29th May, 1919"

On June 1, appropriately it would seem, Ironside organized a King's Birthday Parade. If the British were going to finish up their time in Russia, it would be with plenty of pomp and circumstance! On this occasion, the premiere White Russian force trained by the British, deemed Dyers Battalion of the Slavo-British Legion, presented the colors. The women of Archangel had woven the colors, they were blessed by a bishop of the church and then handed over to a Russian ensign flanked by two bearded Russian soldiers. As they marched by, they were saluted by Russian General Miller, who was impressed and praised the recently trained battalion.

On June 5 General Sadleir-Jackson's brigade arrived in Archangel. Meeting with Sadleir-Jackson, they reminisced on time together in Potchefstroom, South Africa in 1909. Ironside had been a brigade major in the cavalry and Sadleir-Jackson commanded a squadron of 9th Lancers. Ironside saw him as a "hard-riding, hard-fighting officer of independent and determined character." In France he commanded an infantry brigade and was viewed as resourceful and courageous. The troops he brought to North Russia were volunteers organized as battalions of The Royal Fusiliers. He also brought a battery of mountain howitzers.

Ironside's explained his orders had come in by wire the day before from the war department:

"1. *Our latest information indicates that Admiral Kolchak maintains his intention to capture Viatka. If this were done it would probably entail the Bolsheviks abandoning the whole railway as far as Kotlas. However, in view of the reverses he has suffered in South Russia, you must face the possibility of his offensive being delayed in the North, or seriously weakened, and therefore be prepared to modify your plan accordingly.*

2. In any case it is considered that as soon as the necessary means are available, a hard blow should be struck at the Bolsheviks and you should make all preparations for doing so."

Ironside wired back assuring the war department that, with Sadleir-Jackson's brigade and a White Russian unit, he would begin an offensive on the Dvina. He hoped to break the Bolsheviks' front, and if news was good from Kolchak, could press on towards Kotlas. If not, he would be prepared to pull back at any time and create a defensive line as the allies prepared for their final departure from Archangel.

Ironside had remembered Sadleir-Jackson from South Africa as "a most untidy individual" but now found him "quite transformed. With shiny leggings, yellow strappings to his breeches and yellow wash-leather gloves, he looked a real debonair soldier of fortune. Even his moustache had a fiery look."

He gave the general an outline of the current plan. The object would be to get out of Russia with as little fighting as possible. This would mean strengthening the White Russian units based in Archangel so they could carry on the fight when the allies had gone. Sadleir-Jackson's troops, along with White Russians would push back the Bolsheviks' line when the time was right. While preparing, he was to take his 2 battalion commanders up the Dvina to get a feel for where they would be fighting and get to know the commander of the British flotilla.

In the next several weeks Ironside was busy bidding farewell to the troops who had held out through the winter of 1918-19.

He wished that someone had come up with an Arctic medal of some sort, but in the confusion of decisions to abandon North Russia, nothing had been done. Ironside did, however, organize a parade by the docks before the Yanks loaded on their transports. He noted that they had come as "raw and untrained and were leaving as seasoned troops."

As Ironside continued to plan his disengagement strategy, many of the original allied troops, including the Americans to be replaced by the British, Australian and other relief forces, had travelled to Archangel in preparation for leaving Russia. Russians had replaced Yanks on the railroad front on May 7. Companies E and G soon followed them to Archangel. Company K, which had done so much fighting in Kodish, evacuated Kholmogory, and Company F, the last Americans to see action in North Russia in Kitsa in early April, completed its final patrol on May 20.

Company E's Private Donald Carey remembered how some of his troopers had whooped it up a bit on May 21 while passing through the base at Obozerskaya. This included officers like red faced Lt John Baker, who said he had been "for six months as sober as a Philadelphia judge and now I am going to enjoy myself." With a number of drinks under their belts, the officers spent time staggering about and shooting their .45's into the forest.

As the Yanks, the French, the Canadians and the original British troops headed for Archangel, to be replaced by relief forces and White Russians, many worried about what the Bolsheviks' next moves might be. Would they just do teasing attacks or were they preparing a major offensive? It seemed, however, between dealing with Kolchak's forces from the East and the Volunteer Army and other forces pressing from the South, the Bolos were willing to just hold back on major advances till the Allies had gone.

So through May and June a tent city of evacuated Yanks gathered in a district called Economie, north of Archangel.

Here they fought off a new enemy, the swarms of mosquitos of the North Russian summer. As they waited for their transports, they drilled, played baseball and joined in Ironside's parades.

The Yanks also reflected on their time in North Russia and decided to give themselves an identity as the only Americans to have fought in this God forsaken place. They dubbed themselves the Polar Bears and designed a patch with a white polar bear on a blue background, requesting General Richardson to approve it. He did so and had the quartermaster produce patches for the returning veterans to wear.

But before leaving Russia, the Polar Bears faced a growing tension between the Brits and the Yanks. This was not only growing in Archangel, where those relieving them resented the Americans pulling their forces out of the fight, but the Brits in general, were debating all the credit the Yanks were getting for helping end the war. Many of the British felt, by entering the fight after 3 years of slaughter, the Yanks avoided the much higher price in blood and treasure paid by Europeans in the war. These concerns caused a number of spats between the Yanks and the Lineys in the streets of Archangel.

By June 2, however, Companies E, A, G, I and L boarded the perhaps ironically named vessel, Czar, which had brought relief troops and sailed into the White Sea, to the cheers of their countrymen on the dock and the sound of a brass band. An American cruiser blew salutes on its sirens and its sailors cheered, as did the exiting Polar Bears.

The rest of the American forces followed on other ships. The final ship carrying Yanks was the Menominee, on June 15. When it reached Murmansk, Brits on a nearby vessel began yelling taunts at the Americans, and soon metal bolts and fruit and other objects were flying between the two ships. Before the exchange ended, the Yanks had driven the Limeys undercover with their barrage.

But by the next day, the Yanks were on their way out of the icy waters of Murmansk headed for France and a return to their homes in Detroit and throughout the Midwest.

As the Yanks were preparing to get under way, the Canuck Artillery units being replaced by White Russians and British relief gunners, began pulling back to Archangel. Yours truly, Ammon Freeman, and the rest of the 67th Battery, fired two last Salvos at the Bolos and loaded our artillery onto barges for the journey home. The proud unit commanded by Major Arnoldi had served our country well. As he later wrote:

"Many times in France I had talked with other chaps and discussed what a corker of an outfit one could make if one had the choice of men from the whole Corps. Well, I had them. Men from every unit, at least every brigade and including new men from Canada. Picked from a reserve of some 8.500, including the cream of the School of Gunnery. The men were even beyond my expectation and never during our eight months' existence on the front were there any signs of discontent among them. Always game for a fight or a laugh, and it was generally both."

On June 7, the 68th Battery travelled down the Vaga and Dvina to Archangel. The same clouds of river mosquitoes which had swarmed around the Yanks in Economie, reminiscent of those in the Canadian forests, attacked them down the rivers.
Also hidden aboard was the body of Captain Mowat who, despite orders to bury the British and Canadian dead in Russia, his men had decided to spirit away to his home in New Brunswick.

Colonel Sharman paraded our artillery units in the hot midday sun on June 10, the day before our embarkation. General Miller reviewed our Canadian troops, thanking us for our loyal service. Adding to decorations of 4 Canadians earlier in the winter, Sharman received the Order of St Vladimir, and the other officers received the Order of St Anne. Miller also presented the unit with 10 St George medals. This was the only Allied unit to receive this honor. Sharman had our men choose which 10 of us would receive the medals.

Parading before Ironside, who Sharman had come to respect very much (and the feeling was mutual), our troops inspired "Tiny" to remark, "Over and over again the CFA (Canadian Field Artillery) had saved the Force from destruction and the highest traditions of the Canadian Corps had been fully maintained."

Sir Edward Kemp, in a speech to the House of Commons in May, had also lauded our Canadian artillery Brigades with praise:

"Our men have been the backbone of that expedition, because they are physically fit and understood their work, and I have not hesitation in saying they were the best of the troops sent there."

The next day I, 22 officers and 454 other ranks boarded the former Cunard liner Czarista for England. Also departing were Canadians who had flown with the RAF (not including my friend Capt Dugald MacDougal) and Mowat's body. Arriving in Leith, Scotland, we enjoyed 10 days leave. In York we paraded once more on Dominion Day and sailed for Canada on July 4. Not too soon for many in Canada, who, for some time, had been calling for bringing us home.

As in the U.S., Canadian media, legislators, unions and families and friends of the soldiers had been calling for our return for quite a while. With allied forces returning to their families, jobs and homes throughout the world at the end of the Great War, it was completely unacceptable to have these young men stuck in North Russia in an undeclared war through the winter of 1918-19. Finally, the Canadian government had demanded the evacuation of all Canadian forces. But even then, the British War Department, citing security needs, asked for a group of Canadian troops under Colonel Leckie in the Murmansk sector to remain, until they could be relieved by the British relief force. This group was finally relieved on the shores of Lake Onega and sent home.

My dearest wife,

We paraded in York for Dominion Day, which made me proud as a Canadian, and sailed for Canada on July 4th, which made me proud as one with roots in Utah. I will soon be back to you and the dear sweet kiddies.

Gee, it will be great to be back, dear, and stick around the house while you are busy with your multiple duties on the school board, etc. Do you think you can spare me a little time, sweetheart? I'm proud of you, dear: and how I do love you and I dream of you and the kiddies every night. I hope the kiddies will remember me. They must have grown a lot. Kiss them all for me!

I will be gladder than ever that I have kept straight and been a man for their sakes. Conditions have been quite rotten, I can tell you, and it's an impossibility to convince anybody that you are on the straight and narrow. But I never try, just go on and do it, and when I get back to you, sweetheart, then is when I will receive my reward. And it's no small thing to go through this and keep clear. For ten generations Canada will feel the effects of this war.

For the benefits gained, the price has been entirely too high: and people are fast coming to realize that it's a losing game, even if you win.

Keep well and happy, dear: keep smiling and never fear that I pine and live for you always. Kiss all the kiddies and take care of yourself, dearest, until I get there.

Love and kisses, sweetheart.

Your loving,

Am   XXX, XXX Big and little, XXX, xxx

As I rode on the train through the plains of Alberta towards Medicine Hat to meet Florence, I could barely contain my excitement. To while away the time in the last hour before arriving, I pulled out the Book of Mormon, and relished the power and the poetry of Chapter 29 of Alma:

"O that I were an angel, and could have the wish of mine heart, that I might go forth and speak with the trump of God, with a voice to shake the earth, and cry repentance unto every people!

Yea, I would declare unto every soul, as with the voice of thunder, repentance and the plan of redemption, that they should repent and come unto our God, that there might not be more sorrow upon all the face of the earth."

Alma, then, acknowledged he was but a man, and wishing to speak with the power of angels was a sin. He needed to be content with the things given him by God.

Why should he desire to be an angel, to speak to the ends of the earth? The Lord has already granted all nations, in their tongues, the ability to teach God's word and wisdom.

He knew and gloried in what the Lord had commanded him to do. He was to act as an instrument in the hands of God to bring souls to repentance and this was his joy.

He remembered that God had delivered his fathers out of bondage and established the church of the God of Abraham, the God of Isaac, and the God of Jacob. The same God had given him a holy calling, to preach to his people.

But he also was joyful due to the success of his brethren like

Ammon, who had been up to the land of Nephi and done great work. He hoped that God would grant them that they would sit in the kingdom of God and praise him forever.

I caught a cat nap before reaching Medicine Hat and had a brief encounter with my New World Angel, Moroni. He had left the Archangel Michael behind in Russia, of course, and appeared to me as a presence flying above the train, streaking across the plains before reaching the South Saskatchewan River. I remembered an Indian legend I had heard about the name Medicine Hat being based on a mythical river serpent there named Soy-yee-daa-bee, or "the creator," who told a hunter to sacrifice his wife to get mystical powers from a magic hat. It was always interesting to me how each culture has its gods and mythical creatures, as well as sacrificial lambs.

Moroni's voice boomed over the clatter of the train, "You have served your God well, Ammon. Return now to your wife and family and the Mormons of McGrath. You can walk proudly having served your country and your God in the war with the Red Demons!"

I smiled and watched him disappear. I had indeed had visions and guidance on this journey, not unlike that promised to Florence in her patriarchal blessing.

I had to reflect, however, on how the Allies thought they were fighting for God and country and the Bolsheviks thought they were fighting for a fairer world. Considering all the blood and sacrifice endured by both, I wondered whether it was worth the costs.

I surely wasn't going to argue with an angel of God about it, of course, and promptly fell back to sleep.

An excerpt from the Life Sketch of Florence Ida Forsyth Freeman

The town celebrated when Ammon did come home in the fall of 1919, more than 3 years after he left for France. Mae kept the children, and I went to Medicine Hat to meet the troop train when it arrived. Am had saved $100 for each year he was overseas, so had $300. We went out and he bought me a diamond ring. Later, after our son, Marne, was born, I was shopping in Lethbridge, and the stone fell out. I put in a birthstone and never owned a diamond again. We stayed overnight the night Ammon got home and the next day travelled back to McGrath for a turkey dinner and dance for everyone.

Chapter 11

The Last Battle of the Apocalypse

Though things had been relatively quiet on the 5 fronts as outgoing troops were replaced by relief forces, Ironside was wary of letting down his guard against the Bolsheviks. Even with many Bolo deserters coming in and surrendering on the Dvina, saying they were starving out in the forest, he felt that discretion would remain the better part of valor.

Two new Bolo gunboats, with long-range guns more dangerous than the allies' recently acquired 60 pounders, began to give the British flotilla a hard time on the Dvina. They were being directed by observation stations on high ground on the bank of the river.

Ironside realized that the time for a push on the Dvina had come. General Graham, who had commanded the troops during the siege and evacuation of Shenkursk, began an attack on the high ground at Topsa and Troitsa, both on the right bank, and with an advance on the other side of the river. The White Russians were doing a frontal assault, supported by an artillery barrage and two gunboats, Cockchafer and Glowworm. The Hampshires, dragging two mountain howitzers, moved through the forest to attack the Bolos' rear. A flight of seaplanes, including one piloted by Capt MacDougal, was based on a sandbar by Troitsa, acting as spotters for Allied artillery.

The White Russian's were victorious, killing 100 and capturing 500 Bolos. Casualties among the allies were 7 British and 100 Russian's killed or wounded. The Hampshires, however, completely failed in their mission. Hiking 9 miles through the forest to the rear of the enemy, they were startled by a small Bolo patrol approaching them from behind, and retreated back into the forest, failing to engage either the enemy behind *or* in front of them. When they returned to the main body of allied troops, Ironside pulled them off "the line" and had their commander sent back to England.

Though Graham's White Russian attack had not been as successful as it might have been, the Russian patrols pushed forward against the Bolos along the Dvina, finding their defensive line in shatters. The Red gunboats were floating down mines which a British torpedo boat dealt with night and day. Some of the mines were ignited at a distance by rifle fire, and others were blown up with cordite or towed to shallow water.

On July 1 a message arrived for Ironside, who was reviewing the situation on the Dvina, from the Director of Operations at the War Office. It was pessimistic about Kolchak proceeding west towards Kotlas to link up with Ironside's forces in North Russia. There was confusion and were problems between the leaders of the Siberian forces, and little chance they would make progress before winter set in, if at all.

Ironside decided to fly back to Archangel to review the situation with General Miller, who would ultimately take up the slack on any decisions made as the British pulled out of Russia. When they met, the calm, but tired, blue-eyed Russian general took the news well that help was not coming from the Siberian forces. After a few minutes of thought, he asked if Ironside knew when the allied forces needed to leave Archangel.

Ironside replied that a date had not been set, but that he had made it clear to the war office that all troops would need to leave before ice closed the port, probably by the beginning of October. Miller acknowledged that connecting with Siberian troops in Kotlas was out of the question and agreed to outline a plan of the positions his White Russian forces would take in preparation for the exit of the British.

Miller then asked if the British forces planned to completely abandon Archangel and whether they would leave weapons, supplies and transport for Miller to use to continue the fight against the Bolsheviks. Ironside assured him that they would receive what they needed in terms of war materials.

Miller also asked if residents of the region who feared the Bolsheviks could leave as refugees. Ironside said he would confer with the British government, hoping to transport as

135

many refugees as possible with the outgoing troops.

But in response to a query as to whether any of the British troops could be left behind, perhaps as volunteers, to fight for the White Russian cause, Ironside was clear. All allied troops would be out of North Russia before the White Sea froze over.

Knowing he must get back to the forces on the Dvina in their preparations for the final disengaging assaults on the Bolsheviks, Ironside flew back to Troitsa, where barges were transporting Sadleir-Jacksons troops and materials. Busy preparations were in place. Though Ironside was aware that the goal of the operation was no longer a push forward to Kotlas, he kept that information to himself, as the troops prepared for action.

By July 7th, however, another situation with the White Russian forces upset the allied plans. Dyers Battalion of the Slavo British Legion, the pride and joy of the British training program, had arrived on July 4th to prepare to back up one of Sadleir-Jackson's battalions in the coming attack. Travelling upriver, and on inspection when they arrived, they seemed in good spirits.

But on the 5th rifle and Lewis gun fire was heard at the camp where the Dyer B and C companies were billeted. At first it was thought to be an enemy attack, but by 3 am a mutiny by C company was reported, and that some of the troops had gone over to join the Bolsheviks. Worst still, 8 of the mutineers entered the officers' quarters shooting 3 orderlies and killing or wounding 5 British officers. They then also killed 4 Russian officers.

C company fell in, and the mutineers ordered them to join them in going over to the Bolshevik lines. Twenty did so, and later 50 men from Company B also went over to join the Bolos. In all 100 of the Dyer Battalion went with the Reds.

One of the badly wounded British officers, Captain Burr

managed to escape the tent and swim several hundred yards in the river to a boat where he reported the mutiny. Ironside visited him in the hospital the night of the mutiny, praising him for his gallantry and later giving him a Military Cross.

But Ironside, British leadership and General Miller were devastated by the Dyer Battalion's mutiny. It didn't bode well for the future of the White Russian fight against the Bolsheviks.

Ironside was wrestling with when to mount the last battles against the Reds before disengaging and disembarking from North Russia. Repeated mutinies indicated that the longer he waited, the more complications might ensue. After the final attack or attacks, he estimated he would have 3 to 4 weeks to hand off the fronts to the White Russians and evacuate his troops to Archangel for their journey home. Ships were already being loaded with non-essential gear. He finally decided to inform Sadleir-Jackson in mid-August to plan his final assault for mid-September.

Sadleir-Jackson, however, already worried about the White Russians' ability to fight, based on multiple mutinies, and Ironside, were taken aback by yet another mutiny in July 1 in Onega. Seeing the entire Allied right flank had been made vulnerable, Ironside told Sadleir-Jackson to continue planning for his assault, and, when he returned from Archangel, he would set a final target date for the attack. In the meantime, he ordered Sadleir-Jackson, who had begun to completely distrust the White Russians, to work with them and gain their trust.

Returning to Archangel, Ironside learned several of the British officers in Onega had been taken prisoner by the mutineers but had escaped. The base was handed over to the Bolsheviks, but most of the mutineers disappeared into the forest, returned to their homes and destroyed the evidence of their having fought for the Allies.

Ironside met with General Miller, who was preparing a Russian force to retake Onega. He contributed a fresh British machine gun unit to the effort, whose commander was quite pleased that his boys were going get to see some action. Ironside then grabbed 150 Aussies from Sadleir-Jackson's Brigade to take with him by train to Obozerskaya. Here he learned the rebellious Russians in Onega had conspired with Russian companies on the Railroad Front and were about to turn over several blockhouses to the Bolos.

With the help of some Polish troops, the mutiny there was foiled. Ironside thanked the Polish commander for his quick action against the rebels. The commander Count Sollohub, pooh poohed the incident saying "Russians are no good. It is easy to deal with such people." Noting that the Count had all the rebel Russians tied up behind some railway wagons, Ironside had them untied and shipped back to Archangel, and the prison camp at Mudyug Island.

On the 22nd of July, the Bolos attacked the Allies on the Railroad Front, hoping to inspire more mutinies. They were surprised, though, when, instead of mutinous Russians, Aussies with machine guns broke up their attack.

After the mutiny in Onega, and previous mutinies, Ironside began to wonder what more was in store for him. He had just heard, again, from the war office, that Kolchak's advance to the west had been reversed and had definitely become a rout. Should he just launch the final attack in Dvina and get on with it? He decided to fly by seaplane to the Dvina and look at the situation. Before leaving, however, he learned that the Aussies had attacked some of the lead Bolshevik blockhouses on the railroad front. Killing over 30 Bolos in a bayonet charge, they burned several blockhouses and returned to their base, taking no prisoners.

When Ironside arrived on the Dvina, things were quiet. The river level was dropping, which meant fewer of the British and Bolo vessels would be able to maneuver this stretch of the river. This meant Ironside would need to mount an attack soon. The Bolo's were beginning to firm up first and second defensive lines just upriver from the White Russians, who were patrolling regularly to feel out the depth and strength of the enemy forces.

Sadleir Jackson, still upset by the Dyer Battalion's mutiny, didn't really trust the White Russian's intelligence, but, having sent out Brit intelligence officers with their patrols, agreed with Ironside when, at the end of July, he fixed the 10th of August as a tentative date for an attack on the Bolo's front line. If this was successful, it would knock the Bolsheviks back on their heals, giving two or three weeks to evacuate Allied forces to Archangel, and allow the White Russians to fall back to a strong defensive line at the base at Bereznik.

The White Russian Commander Colonel Prince Mourousi, had been identified by Ironside as a potential leader earlier as a private in the Slavo-British Legion. He had become an inspiring commander of his troops under General Miller and had planned a sophisticated attack to drive the Bolos upriver as far as allowed. Ironside, frustrated that he wasn't aware of this leader and his unit's enthusiasm sooner, had to outline what would be modest goals for the attack. The idea would be to break the enemy's lines, but then fall back to well-developed defensive lines in Bereznik, to screen the retreat of the Allied forces to Archangel.

Not only was Colonel Mourousi disappointed by the limited goals of the attack, but his Russian troops were relegated to preparing the defense of Bereznik, and Sadleir Jackson's troops would be carrying out the attack. Using the Russian's plan to the letter, on Aug 10, the attack went forward. The plan had been to do a frontal attack with ¼ of the White forces, with ¾ attacking on the flanks and rear. Each unit was to attack and keep attacking with no mercy. The units, including the gunboats HMS Glowworm and Cockchafer, were in communication with field wireless or cables. An observation balloon, manned by the Navy, spotted for the artillery and followed the battle. The Cockchafer would bombard the enemy ashore and the Glowworm would defend against enemy gunboats. The attack, 2 miles wide on each bank of the Dvina, and 10 miles deep, was, from Ironside's perspective, a masterful plan. Mourousi had even planned to have all communications done in English, rather than Russian, to keep the Bolos in the dark as to the Allied moves.

At dawn of August 10, the attack began, and completely defeated the Bolshevik forces. Heavy losses were incurred by the Bolos, especially in the rear. One Bolo gunboat was destroyed, and two were beached and captured by the advancing Brits. 3,000 Red prisoners were taken. Having incurred casualties of 145 killed or wounded, the Allies had succeeded in "breaking the Bolsheviks' lines" in preparation for the retreat from North Russia.

Lord Henry Rawlinson, appointed Commander In Chief to oversee the Allied evacuation of North Russia, both in Murmansk and Archangel, left England August 4th arriving on the 11th, after meeting briefly with General Maynard in Murmansk. One of the most respected generals in France, Rawlinson had commanded the 4th Army on the Somme and earned much respect and many medals, including the Russian Order of St George during the Great War. Ironside, somewhat surprised another general was brought in for the evacuation, had met him briefly during the war and was looking forward to working with him.

Meeting with Rawlinson when his ship arrived at the quay in Archangel, Ironside strode into the ship's smoking room and was greeted by the general, standing "in front of the electric stove, his legs wide apart and his hands clasped behind his back, his head thrust forward and a smile on his face. He put me at once at my ease by addressing me by my nickname, "Tiny." He shook me warmly by the hand and thanked me for sending so clear an explanation of the situation. There started from that moment a close and, to me, a very precious friendship which lasted until the day of his death in India, where he was serving as Commander in Chief."

In preparation for meeting that evening with the Governor-General, General Miller, Rawlinson questioned Ironside on the Allies' situation in North Russia. He was particularly concerned about the details of the mutinies. Ironside felt that discipline was the key to dealing with the potentially mutinous troops. The Russian artillery and machine gunners, with training and discipline, had remained faithful. They had even fired on their own mutineers. Having been an artillery officer, Ironside alluded to the "Spirit of the Gun."

Rawlinson, still concerned about the potential of mutinies, grinned and quipped, "Oh, I see. Once a Gunner, always a Gunner!"

Ironside prepared Rawlinson for the meeting with Miller, pointing out that the General was extremely loyal to the Allies, and would do everything that was asked of him in carrying out the military operations needed for the evacuation. Knowing that Rawlinson's French wasn't that great, he arranged a Russian translator for the meeting.

That evening, Rawlinson met patiently with Miller, listening carefully during the translations. He began by arguing that having Miller try and defend both Murmansk and Archangel from the Bolsheviks was too much to take on. He offered to help transport all the White Russian forces to Murmansk, to concentrate his forces.

After a pause, Miller thanked "Rawly," but declined his offer. He felt that he would not be honoring his obligation to defend the region by retreating to Murmansk. He noted that, even if he was able to only hold off the Bolsheviks for a short time in Archangel, in the big picture, that would buy time and give others the opportunity to press forward on other fronts in the civil war.

Getting down to nuts and bolts, Miller asked if a date for withdrawal of all the British troops had been set. Rawlinson said that, at this moment, September 1 was the date. Grimacing, Miller argued that he was planning certain offenses with his troops which would help the British with their evacuation. Agreeing to move the date to September 10, Rawlinson was firm in noting that the British troops could not be expected to assist in Miller's operations.

Ironside was given carte blanche to supply Miller with all the supplies, ammunition and weapons they requested, as long as they were already in inventory in Russia and did not require additional material transported from England.

Having concluded their discussion, Ironside was glad he didn't have to be the one explaining to Miller the fate he faced. Rawlinson had treated the general kindly and respectfully, but when Miller had almost begged for more resources and support, lines needed to be drawn. Also, realistically, most of the Allies felt, with good reason, that Miller and his White Russian forces, would likely face defeat, before long, by the Bolshevik forces.

Later, in reviewing Miller's plans for attacks against the Bolos during the evacuation, he found them overly ambitious for the number of troops the general commanded. There were unclear objectives on the Dvina, as the enemy had not re-formed a line there. He suggested, and Miller agreed, to limit his offensives to the Railroad Front, Seletskoe on the Emtsa, and later actions in Onega as well as realistic lines of defense on the Dvina.

Mapping this out as a White Russian defense line from West to East, that would be Onega-Pletsetskaya-Tarasevo-Beresnik. Having these points fortified by the Russians, the British would do a five-stage withdrawal to the "Inner Defense Line of Archangel." Sadleir-Jackson's Dvina force would set the pace of the withdrawal.

Before the final disengaging battles in Archangel province, our friend Dugald MacDougall ran into trouble out on the Dvina. After supporting the fighting during the summer on the lower Dvina with his seaplane based in Beresnik and Troitsa, he had joined some friends for dinner aboard the HMS Glowworm which was preparing, with the HMS Cockchafer, to relieve two other of the British gunboats on river duty. Near Beresnik on the night of August 24, after a great dinner, Dugald and Glowworm's acting commander, Sebald Green, a lieutenant with the Irish Guard and a Russian interpreter, were enjoying drinks on the bridge. They suddenly noticed a loaded barge, the NT 396 Edinburgh, had caught on fire. Apparently the crew had not put out their galley fires adequately.

Green ordered the Glowworm to pull up to the Edinburgh and the crew began uncoiling fire hoses on the bow and fighting the fire. The Cockchafer also began pulling up to the other side of the barge, preparing to assist as necessary.

Not realizing that the barge was loaded with 70 tons of high explosives, Dugald and those on the bridge, other sailors on the Glowworm and people on the shore, stared in awe as the flames grew and the sailors fought the fire.

Suddenly a huge explosion sent a wall of flames high into the night sky. Almost instantaneously, second and third massive explosions lit up the countryside followed by a huge roar and shockwave sending debris out to a full mile radius.

Rescue crews rowed to the Glowworm from the shore. Rescuers found the superstructure scorched and bent and debris and bodies were everywhere. Firefighters were killed at their hoses. Rescuers found several crewmen alive but in shock on their way to the bridge. When they reached the bridge MacDougall and all others were dead or beyond help. Commander Green was still alive and was taken the Beresnik hospital but died an hour later. The Cockchafer pulled up to the Glowworm and continued with rescue efforts.

Before the fire was quelled, 24 of the 54 Glowworm crewmembers and guests were killed by burns, concussion of the explosions or flying debris. All were buried in Beresnik. And our friend Dugald, who had volunteered to stay on with the RAF and help our White Russian friends push back the Bolos, when he, as a Canadian, could have left earlier in the summer, ended his young life.

General Miller's attacks on the Railroad and Seletskoe (Emtsa River) began with great success on August 29th. His White Russian troops, unlike the previous mutineers, stayed loyal and committed, aggressively assaulting the enemy forces. He was supported by RAF biplanes bombing enemy positions and some of Sadleir-Jackson's Aussie Brigade on the railroad, with another aggressive bayonet attack which terrified the Bolos. Miller followed up with an attack and re-capture of Onega on September 10th, as the British began the withdrawal of all their troops.

As the water level of the Dvina continued to drop, two of the British Monitors ran aground near the yacht *Kathleen*, which served as Sadleir-Jackson's headquarters. They threw ballast overboard on all vessels and blasted the channel, and still couldn't move downstream. The *Kathleen* finally powered her way across the bar, but the two Monitors were destroyed to keep them out of the hands of the Bolsheviks. As the British moved downstream, they mined the Dvina heavily with magnetic and other explosives. This kept the Bolsheviks from chasing the retreating British troops down the river.

By September 23rd, all of the British forces were in position in the "Inner Defense Line" in Archangel. The troops began to be ferried down to the mouth of the Dvina in smaller vessels, where they were delivered to the transport ships.

On August 26, Ironside arrived for tea and to spend his last night in Russia on Admiral Sir John Green's yacht, tied up at the dock near the great cathedral. They watched the sun go down and the lights go out in Archangel, as a curfew had been called. The city was quiet as they enjoyed dinner, hoping their luck would continue on the evacuation. Piskoff had already left with the Canadians, but Ironside's driver, Kostia, slept aboard the boat. Kostia, now 17 years old, would evacuate with Ironside and serve with the general for many years. As a son of a rural Russian farmer, Kostia was virtually adopted as Ironside's driver, and became like a son to him. In later years he travelled with him to Hungary, Anatolia, North Persia and India. He ended up serving in the Royal Tank Corps in WW II and working in intelligence in Berlin after that war.

By mid-morning the next day, General Miller and his ADC, Count Hamilton, walked down the pier to the yacht. Looking depressed, they were piped on board by the Admiral and a Naval guard. Inspecting the contingent, General Miller shook the hand of the lieutenant in charge, praising the guard in Russian.

He turned to Ironside and shook hands. They conversed awkwardly for twenty minutes. Then Miller thanked Ironside and the admiral for all they had done for Russia and asked that they present his compliments to Lord Rawlinson and the British government. Ironside thanked him for his efforts to support the safe evacuation of the allied forces. He noted that he would always admire Miller's loyalty to Russia and courtesy to Ironside under trying circumstances in Archangel. Ironside wished him well, and Miller bowed deeply before the guard returned to pipe him ashore.

As Miller and Count Hamilton slowly walked down the pier, Ironside hoped they would turn and wave goodbye. But not looking back, they disappeared into the city to meet their fate.

The yacht cast off into the channel, lowering it's ensign in respect as it passed the cathedral. Ironside mused one more time on the somber mural of the last judgment as the church faded from view.

Heading downriver on the Dvina they passed the large Archangel sawmills. Ironside reflected on how the inhabitants of Archangel had neither cheered the Allied forces when they arrived, nor had they even turned out to bid them farewell when they left.

When informed by the admiral that all the troops had been loaded aboard their transports, Tiny was piped over the side and was ferried to the Czaritza. The crews of the Admiral's yacht, echoed by the troops aboard the transports, gave hearty cheers as they set sail for England.

I was at home in McGrath when the Brits left Archangel, but the night they set sail, asleep in my bed, the Archangel Michael returned to my dreams. I watched him flying above the White Sea as the Czarista sailed to the west. Waving Ironside and the troops goodbye, he flew back to the domed church in Archangel. Lighting upon the parapet, he stood and gazed out over the city. All knowing and all seeing, he knew the Bolsheviks would retake Archangel in the Spring. Below him at that moment he saw General Miller solemnly walking by, staring sadly at the painting of the Last Judgement.

I had been home with Florence and the kiddies for several months. I was happy to be feeling the love of my wife and family more than I could have imagined. With time with them, getting back to work and getting reacquainted with my friends in McGrath, I had very little time to read. Finally, one night, I picked up the Mormon holy scriptures again, this time The Doctrines and Covenants, 21-25, that felt like it caught the power and vision of our beliefs.

"And the voice of Michael, the archangel; the voice of Gabriel,

and of Raphael, and of divers angels, from Michael or Adam down to the present time, all declaring their dispensations, their rights, their keys, their honors, their majesty and glory, and the power of their priesthood; giving line upon line, precept upon precept; here a little, and there a little, giving us consolation by holding forth that which is to come, confirming our hope!

Brethren, shall we not go on in so great a cause? Go forward and not backward. Courage, brethren; and on, on to the victory! Let your hearts rejoice and be exceedingly glad. Let the earth break forth into singing. Let the dead speak forth anthems of eternal praise to the King Immanuel, who hath ordained, before the world was, that which would enable us to redeem them out of their prison; for the prisoners shall go free.

Let the mountains shout for joy, and all ye valleys cry aloud; and all ye seas and dry lands tell the wonders of your Eternal King! And ye river, and brooks and rills, flow down with gladness. Let the woods and all the trees of the field praise the Lord; and ye solid rocks weep for joy! And let the sun, moon, and the morning stars sing together, and let all the sons of God shout for joy! And let the eternal creation declare his name forever and ever! And again I say how glorious is the voice we hear from heaven, proclaiming in our ears, glory and salvation, and honor, and immortality, and eternal life; kingdoms, principalities, and powers!

Behold, the great day of the Lord is at hand; and who can abide the day of his coming, and who can stand when he appeareth? For he is like a refiner's fire, and like fuller's soap; and he shall sit as a refiner and purifier of silver, and he shall purify the sons of Levi, and purge them as gold and silver, that they may offer unto the Lord an offering of righteousness. Let us, therefore, as a church and a people, and as Latter-day Saints, offer unto the Lord an offering in righteousness; and let us present in his holy temple, when it is finished, a book containing the records of our dead, which shall be worthy of all acceptation.

I am, as ever, your humble servant and never deviating friend, Joseph Smith"

But heck, I am just a not-to-perfect Jack Mormon from McGrath, Alberta, and not a great one to speak about our beliefs.

Within a year another son was born to the Freeman family, who we named after the turning point battle of the Great War (the Marne) and, his middle name, Leroy, was in honor of my best friend Roy Harris, who had died at Vimy Ridge. These names seemed more appropriate for a Canadian than Archangel, Tulgas, Shenkursk, Vistafka or Kodish, from my time in North Russia.

We lived a few more years in McGrath, but, despite my best efforts to quell my Jack Mormon habits, drinking, smoking and occasionally chasing the young ladies did not end after my return from the war. Finally, I got myself and 5 other teachers fired from the elementary school in McGrath for a very non-Mormon party we had one night.

Losing my job, but somehow not losing Florence and the kids, we moved to East Center Street in Bountiful, Utah, to take care of her mother who had cancer. I worked again as a teacher, and later did painting, carpentry and other odd jobs. Florence was active in the church and became a teacher in the Relief Society. I, of course, never quite became the kind of Mormon she and my folks would have hoped.

But we raised a smart and intelligent family of 7 kids, whose own children and grandchildren have spread out around the world, and of whom we were very proud. All our boys served in the next Great War, World War II. We honored their generation's service like our generation did ours.

I finish telling this tale of my time in Russia, though, so my grandchildren and their children can share it and think about how we can create a world where the various legions will stop battling in an emulation of the Apocalypse.

Amen.

Ammon Freeman

Post-Script

Many years later, in the 1960s, Florence and I visited Marne and his wife Maxine's home in what later became the Silicon Valley of California. We were watching TV one night with their two sons when a story on an anti-war demonstration against the Vietnam War came on. Long haired protestors were calling for peace and ending the war in which the U.S. was supporting one group of Vietnamese, who were anti-communists, against another, who were communists. Florence was upset and made a comment about how unpatriotic it was to protest a war in which American soldiers were fighting.

As I watched the demonstrators, I remembered back to when Canadians and Americans were protesting back home while we fought the communists in Russia. I sympathized with these young people's efforts to bring their countrymen home. I also felt it was ironic that, many years later, the same battles were being fought.

I didn't say anything, as I long ago learned it best not to argue with Florence. But I smiled and hoped Marne's sons would be smart enough not to go off and fight for "king and country" in Vietnam.

Marne's oldest son was named after him, and still carried, in his name, the heritage of the battle of the Marne and the death of my friend Roy in the battle of Vimy Ridge. But his youngest son, Laurence Winston, was named after the great British actor, Laurence Olivier and Winston Churchill, the architect of the Allied fight against the Bolsheviks at the end of the Great War. A bit ironic, also, I thought.

Another irony, though, is that the rifle we and the Bolos used in Russia, the Mosin-Nagant, invented in 1891, and first used in the Russo-Japanese war in 1904, was still being used in wars throughout the 20th Century. They were being produced by Remington and Westinghouse for the Tsar in WW I, but after the Bolshevik revolution the Bolos had plenty in stock, and refused to pay for them, nearly putting the two companies into bankruptcy. But the U.S. government bought the rest, providing them to the those of us fighting the Bolsheviks in North Russia and Siberia, as well as the White Russian armies. Used throughout World War II, they were back to killing French, American and Australian soldiers by the Viet Minh and Viet Cong in the Vietnam War.

I was relieved when neither my grandson Marne Leroy Jr nor Laurence Winston had to face them in Vietnam!

And again,

Amen.

Ammon Freeman

"O THAT I WERE AN ANGEL, AND COULD HAVE THE WISH OF MINE HEART, THAT I MIGHT GO FORTH AND SPEAK WITH THE TRUMP OF GOD, WITH A VOICE TO SHAKE THE EARTH, AND CRY REPENTANCE UNTO EVERY PEOPLE.

YEA, I WOULD DECLARE UNTO EVERY SOUL, AS WITH THE VOICE OF THUNDER, REPENTANCE AND THE PLAN

*OF REDEMPTION, THAT THEY SHOULD REPENT AND
COME UNTO OUR GOD, THAT THERE MIGHT NOT BE
MORE SORROW UPON ALL THE FACE OF THE EARTH.*

*AND BEHOLD, I AM A MAN, AND DO SIN IN MY WISH; FOR
I OUGHT TO BE CONTENT WITH THE THINGS WHICH THE
LORD HATH ALOTTED UNTO ME.*

*I OUGHT NOT TO HARROW UP IN MY DESIRES, THE
FIRM DECREE OF A JUST GOD, FOR I KNOW THAT HE
GRANTETH UNTO MEN ACCORDING TO THEIR DESIRE,
WHETHER IT BE UNTO DEATH OR UNTO LIFE; YEA, I
KNOW THAT HE ALLOTTETH UNTO MEN, YEA,
DECREETH UNTO THEM DECREES WHICH ARE
UNALTERABLE, ACCORDING TO THEIR WILLS,
WHETHER THEY BE UNTO SALVATION OR UNTO
DESTRUCTION.*

*YEA, AND I KNOW THAT GOOD AND EVIL HAVE COME
BEFORE ALL MEN; HE THAT KNOWETH NOT GOOD
FROM EVIL IS BLAMELESS; BUT HE THAT KNOWETH
GOOD AND EVIL, TO HIM IT IS GIVEN ACCORDING TO
HIS DESIRES, WHETHER HE DESIRETH GOOD OR EVIL,
LIFE OR DEATH, JOY OR REMORSE OF CONSCIENCE.*

*NOW SEEING THAT I KNOW THESE THINGS, WHY
SHOULD I DESIRE MORE THAN TO PERFORM THE WORK
TO WHICH I HAVE BEEN CALLED?*

*WHY SHOULD I DESIRE THAT I WERE AN ANGEL, THAT I
COULD SPEAK UNTO ALL THE ENDS OF THE EARTH?
BOOK OF MORMON ALMA CHAPTER 29*

When I knew my time on earth was growing short, I lay in my
bed on the back porch of our house in Bountiful, Utah.
Florence had made up a clean bed and helped me bathe the
night before. She joked how she didn't know if she could bathe

me regularly. I assured her I would be perfectly well in the morning. Then she looked worried when I took my Book of Mormon to bed. She knew I recently had taken to liking Zane Grey westerns.

Before falling asleep I opened to Mormon, Chapter 8. Perhaps I thought by reading some of Moroni's writing, I might bring back my old friend, one more time.

"Behold I, Moroni, do finish the record of my father, Mormon. Behold, I have but few things to write, which things have been commanded by my father.

And now it came to pass that after the great and tremendous battle at Cumorah, the Nephites who had escaped into the country southward were hunted by the Lamanites, until they were all destroyed.

And my father also was killed by them, and I even remain alone to write the sad tale of the destruction of my people. But behold, they are gone, and I fulfil the commandment of my father. And whether they will slay me, I know not.

Therefore I will write and hide the records in the earth; and whither I go it mattereth not.

Behold, my father hath made this record, and he hath written the intent thereof. And behold, I would write it also if I had room upon the plates, but I have not; and ore I have none, for I am alone. My father hath been slain in battle, and all my kinsfolk, and I have not friends nor whither to go; and how long the Lord will suffer that I may live I know not.

Behold, four hundred years have passed away since the coming of our Lord and Savior.

And behold, the Lamanites have hunted my people, the

Nephites, down from city to city and from place to place, even until they are no more; and great has been their fall; yea, great and marvelous is the destruction of my people, the Nephites.

And behold, it is the hand of the Lord which hast done it. And behold also, the Lamanites are at war one with another; and the whole face of the land is one continual round of murder and bloodshed; and no one knoweth the end of war.

And now, behold, I say no more concerning them, for there are none save it be the Lamanites and robbers that do exist upon the face of the land.

And there are none that do know the true God save it be the disciples of Jesus, who did tarry in the land until the wickedness of the people was so great that the Lord would not suffer them to remain with the people; and whether they be upon the face of the land no man knoweth.

And whoso receiveth this record and shall not condemn it because of its imperfections which are in it, the same shall know of greater things than these. Behold, I am Moroni, and were it possible, I would make all things known unto you.

Behold, I make an end of speaking concerning this people. I am the son of Mormon, and my father was a descendant of Nephi.

I am the same who hideth up this record unto the Lord; the plates thereof are of no worth, because of the commandment of the Lord. For he truly saith that no one shall have them to get gain; but the record thereof is of great worth; and those shall bring it to light, him will the Lord bless.

For none can have power to bring it to light save it be given him of God; for God wills that it shall be done with an eye single to his glory, or the welfare of the ancient and long dispersed covenant people of the Lord.

And blessed be he that shall bring this thing to light; for it shall be brought out of darkness unto light, according to the word of God; yet it shall be brought out of the earth, and it shall shine forth out of the darkness, and come unto the knowledge of the people; and it shall be done by the power of God."

As I finished reading, I fell asleep and was immediately in the presence of the Angel Moroni, again blowing his holy trumpet in the sky. White light emanated from his robes and his body, filling time and space with luminescence. As I flew, spinning up as if in a hurricane of light, I saw, too, Moroni and the Archangel Michael waving goodbye, and heard the song of our forefathers singing:

"Come, come, ye saints, no toil nor labor fear;
But with joy wend your way.
Though hard to you this journey may appear,
grace shall be as your day.
Tis better far for us to strive
our useless cares from us to drive;
do this, and joy your hearts will swell -
All is well! All is well!"

"Why should we mourn or think our lot is hard?
'Tis not so; all is right.
Why should we think to earn a great reward
if we now shun the fight?
Gird up your loins; fresh courage take,
our God will never us forsake;
and soon we'll have this tale to tell-
all is well! All is well!
"We'll find the place which God for us prepared,
in His house full of light,
where none shall come to hurt or make afraid;
there the saints will shine bright.
We'll make the air with music ring,
shout praises to our God and King;
above the rest these words we'll tell,
all is well! All is well!"

"And should we die before our journey's through,
happy day! All is well!
We then are free from toil and sorrow, too;
with the just we shall dwell!
But if our lives are spared again
to see the Saints their rest obtain,
oh, how we'll make this chorus swell-
all is well! All is well!"

Looking down on the porch bed I could see my body lying, with Florence leaning over me. She kissed me softly and quoted what Evangeline said to Gabriel, "All is ended now, the hope and the joy and the sorrow. All the deep pain and the constant anguish of patience." As she raised my lifeless head to her bosom she added, "Father, thank thee."

The End

About the Author

The author of The Archangel Invasion, Marne L Mercer, has been researching the Allied intervention in Russia for many years. In 2014 he toured historical sites in Archangel and visited battlefields in Tulgas, Mudyug Island, the Railroad Front and Vistafka.

Marne is the grandson of a Mormon from Canada, Ammon Mercer. The letters home from Ammon Freeman in this book were based on letters home from Ammon Mercer to his wife Florence from England and France during WW I. Ammon fought in the battle of Vimy Ridge where his best friend, Leroy Harris, was killed and he was wounded. He spent the rest of the war in hospitals in England. These letters were edited to reflect the experiences of a fictional Ammon Freeman in France and Northern Russia.

The Archangel Invasion Bibliography

Ace of Spies: The True Story of Sidney Reilly, Andrew Cook, The History Press, 2004

Adventures of a British Master Spy: The Memoirs of Sidney Reilly, Sidney Reilly, Biteback Publishing, 2014

Allied Intervention in Russia 1918-1919: And the Part Played by Canada, **Routledge Library Editions: The Russian Civil War Book 4,** John Swettenham, 1967

Allied Intervention in Russia 1918-1920: General W.P. Richardson & His Role in Withdrawal of The American Troops from North Russia, Skipper Steely, Steely Mini Book History

Series,

The Allied Intervention in Russia, 19-18-1919: The diplomacy of chaos, Ian C.D. Moffat, Palgrave Macmillan, 2015

America's Secret War Against Bolshevism: U.S. Intervention in the Russian Civil War, 1917-1920, David Foglesong, University of North Carolina Press, 1995

Always With Honor: The Memoirs of General Wrangel, Pyotr Wrangel, Mystery Grove Publishing

Archangel: The American War With Russia, John Cudahy, Lume Books, 1924

Archangel 1918-1919, Gen. Ironsides, The Navy and Military Press, Ltd., CPI Antony Rowe, Eastbourne, 2007.

The Book of Mormon, Church of Jesus Christ of Latter-Day Saints, Intellectual Reserve, Inc, 1981,2013

Canadians in Russia 1918-1919, Roy MacLaren, Macmillan of Canada, Toronto, 1976

Churchill's Crusade: The British Invasion of Russia 1918-1920, Clifford Kinvig, Hambledon Continuum, London, 2006

Churchill and the Archangel Fiasco (Russia and the Allies, 1917-1920), Michael Kettle, Routledge, 1992

Churchill's Secret War with Lenin: British and Commonwealth Military Intervention in The Russian Civil War, 1918-20, Damien Wright, Helion and Company, 2017

The Decision to Intervene, George F Kennan, Princeton University Press, 1953

Essential Works of Lenin: "What Is to Be Done?" and Other Writings, Vladimir Ilyich Lenin, Bantam Books, 1966

Fighting the Bolsheviks: The Russian War Memoir of Private First Class Donald E. Carey, U.S. Army, 1918-1919, Neil G. Carey, Presidio Press, Novato, CA, 1997

From Victoria to Vladivostok: Canada's Siberian Expedition, 1917-19, Benjamin Isitt, UBC Press, Vancouver-Toronto, 1978.

History of the American Expedition Fighting the Bolsheviks: US Intervention in Soviet Russia 1918-1919, Capt. Joel R Moore, Lt Harry H Meade, and Lt Lewis E Jahns, Red and Black Publishers, St Petersburg, FLA, 1920

The House by the Dvina: A Russian Childhood, Eugenie Fraser, Mainstream Publishing, 1984

Intervention in Russia 1918-1920: A Cautionary Tale, Miles Hudson, Leo Cooper, South Yorkshire, 1984

Ironside: The Authorized Biography of Field Marshal Lord Ironside, Edmund Ironside, The History Press, 2018

Last Train Over Rostov Bridge, Captain Marion Aten and Arthur Ormont, Julian Messner Inc, 1961

LDS Triple Combination: The Book of Mormon, Doctrine and Covenants, The Pearl of Great Price,

Memoirs of a British Agent, R.H. Bruce Lockhart, Frontline Books, 2011

A Michigan Polar Bear Confronts the Bolsheviks: A War Memoir, Godfrey Anderson, William B. Eerdmans Publishing Company, Grand Rapids, Michigan, 2010.

N. R. E. F. 16th Brigade, C. F. A., 67th and 68th Batteries in North Russia, September 1918 to June 1919. There is a copy of this 55 page history in the University of Michigan collection that can be downloaded.

Quartered in Hell: The Story of American North Russian Expeditionary Force 1918-1919, Dennis Gordon, Doughboy Historical Society, Missoula, MT, 1982

Russian Sideshow: America's Undeclared War, 1918-1920, Robert L Willett, Brassey's, Inc., Washington DC, 2003

Stamping Out The Virus: Allied Intervention in the Russian Civil War, 1918-1920, Perry Moore, Schiffer Military History, Atglen, PA, 2002.

The Decision to Intervene: Soviet American Relations, 1917-1920, George F Kennan, Princeton University Press, Princeton, New Jersey, 1958

The Ignorant Armies, E.M Halliday, Award Books, New York City, 1958

The Master and Margarita: 50th Anniversary Edition, Mikhail Bulgakov, Penguin Books, 2001

The Midnight War: The American Intervention in Russia 1918-1920, Richard Goldhurst, McGraw Hill Books, New York, 1978.

The Pale Horse, Boris Savinkov,

The Polar Bear Expedition: The Heroes of America's Forgotten Invasion of Russia 1918-1919, James Carl Nelson, William Morrow, Harper Collins Publishers, 1019

The Private War of Sidney Reilly: A Tale of Revolutionary Russia, Allan Torrey, A.T Chesterton Publisher, 2014

Red Dusk and the Morrow: Adventures and Investigations in Red Russia, Paul Dukes, Good Press, 2019

The Romance of Company "A", 339 Infantry, A.N.R.E.F., Dorothea York, McIntyre Printing, Detroit, MI, 1923

The Russian Civil Wars 1916-1926: Ten Years That Shook The World, Jonathon D Smele, Oxford University Press, 2015

Trailing the Bolsheviki: Twelve Thousand Miles with the Allies in Siberia, Carl W Ackerman, Charles Scribners Sons, 1919

Russia in Flames: War, Revolution, Civil War 1914-1921, Laura Englestein, Oxford University Press, 2018

Russian Revolution: Concise History From Beginning to End, Hourly History, 2016

Stillborn Crusade: The Tragic Failure of Western Intervention in the Russian Civil War 1918-1920, Ilya Somin, Routledge, 1996

The United States Intervention in North Russia 1918, 1919 The Polar Bear Odyssey, Roger Crownover, The Edwin Mellen Press, Lewiston New York, 2001

The World Crisis Volume 3 and 4, 1916-1918 and The Aftermath, Winston Churchill, Rosetta Books, 2013

When Hell Froze Over, E.M. Halliday, I-Books, New York, 1958 (originally published as Ignorant Armies).

When the United States Invaded Russia: Woodrow Wilson's Siberian Disaster, Carl J Richard, Rowman and Littlefield, 2013

White Armies of Russia: A Chronicle of Counter-Revolution and Allied Intervention, George Stewart, Naval and Military Press DTD,

White Guard, Mikhail Bulgakov, Yale University Press, New Haven, 2008

Why did we go to Russia, Harry J. Costello, 1920

Wolfhounds and Polar Bears: The American Expeditionary Force in Siberia, 1918-1920, John M. House, University of Alabama Press, 2016

Made in the USA
Columbia, SC
29 November 2021